Renascence

Alliance Series 1-6

By Alma Nilsson

WAR

Admiral Tir of the Alliance warship *Refa* looked across the virtual projection of the battle they were currently engaged in with the Jahay and said to his first officer, "Save the humans. It would be such a waste to let the women die."

Captain Zan nodded and began giving orders to bring the small human starship *Dakota* into one of their docking bays. He instructed some guards and medics to attend to them.

Admiral Tir stopped him, "Don't waste our resources on the men, heal only the women, let the men die if they are going to die. Then put them all into the brig. We will send the women back to the Alliance on the next supply ship." The Alliance was the largest and most advanced civilization in the galaxy, but they were suffering from a demographics problem and needed genetically compatible women. The only other compatible women in the galaxy were human.

Three hours later, the battle was won and after Admiral Tir had finished all the necessary reports, he decided to check in on his human prisoners. He was not completely unfamiliar with the *Dakota* as its captain had led many Alliance supply ships into danger and even managed to destroy two Alliance ships during the war. It was an impressive feat given that the *Dakota* was a completely inferior ship.

He first went to the brig. When he entered, the guards saluted him. He acknowledged them and silently looked over the humans. He was looking for their captain. He hated that humans did not identify their ranks with clearly marked uniforms. He loathed having to ask, "Which one of you," he addressed the women who were being held in a separate cell from the men, "is Captain Rainer?"

All the women looked up and then a beautiful, dark-skinned woman answered him, "She is not with us. Maybe you had her killed?"

He ignored the anger in the woman's voice and did not answer her. He did not expect kindness, but at the very least gentility for not killing them. He ignored the woman who had spoken to him. He then went directly to his ship's sickbay. He walked through the different colored humans in varying states of health and looked for his chief medical officer, Doctor Siu.

"Is their captain here? I would like to speak to her."

Doctor Siu pointed to a medical bed in the back, "She is there. Red uniform. She hit her head, it looks worse than it is."

Admiral Tir stood over her. He could see from the read out above her medic bed that she was not asleep but just had closed her eyes. "Captain Rainer, I am Admiral Tir of the Alliance. You and your crew are our prisoners."

Kara opened her eyes and was surprised to see a good-looking, grey-skinned Alliance man with long black hair and striking green eyes looking down at her. She never imagined Alliance citizens to be good-looking, but this man was handsome. "Thank you for saving us, for the moment anyway, I didn't think the Alliance took prisoners, Admiral."

"We are making an exception for the woman who was brave enough to constantly disrupt our supply lines with your completely inferior ship." Humans had a reputation for being some of the most beautiful species in the galaxy with all their colors and soft skin, but he had never met a human before, so he was intrigued by her brown hair and brown eyes. He had the urge to reach out and touch her hair, but he resisted.

Kara smiled, "I am glad that I made an impression." Human ships were nothing in the galaxy. When the Jahay had forced the humans to join this war against the Alliance, she knew they would probably die, but she would at least do what humans had become experts at, guerrilla warfare, before they met their end. She and her entire crew knew that they would meet their ends in this war, there was no doubt about it. She had not counted on being saved by an Alliance ship though, by a particularly handsome Admiral. She was intrigued then, wondering what he really wanted from them. She was trying to read his face but could find nothing there. Before she could ask, he was gone.

He touched her shoulder as a reply to statement, as he could not help himself, and then left without saying anything more. She had first made an impression on him for being a brilliant strategist and now being so young and attractive. He used to feel sorry for anyone who would have to marry a human, but now he was beginning to reconsider his prejudice against the human women.

Later that afternoon, Admiral Tir had the guards bring Captain Rainer to him in his conference room so he could talk to her privately. When she entered, he was intoxicated by her scent and although she looked tired and dirty, he still found her very attractive. He was fascinated by her golden skin and her pink lips. Her uniform was tight and showed off all her curves. It had a zipper down the front and all he wanted to do in that first minute of looking at her was to unzip it slowly to reveal her naked curves and check where else she may be pink on her body.

Captain Rainer was struck again with how handsome and tall Admiral Tir was, well over two meters. She had not realized before, as everyone looks tall when you are lying down. He had endless, thick black hair that he wore loose down his back that she suddenly longed to run her fingers through it. She took in his black uniform and colorful jewelry which she knew denoted rank and then her eyes rested on his sword and she was brought back to reality then that she was his prisoner and that they were not meeting under equal terms. Their eyes met, and she saw how he was looking at her, "Is this the first time you have ever seen a human?" She was used to this. Most of the galaxy was made up of ugly species, humans were considered the most beautiful, but were also only genetically compatible with Alliance citizens. Humans normally did not find Alliance citizens attractive because they had grey skin, but Kara thought to herself, *there is a first for everything.*

Admiral Tir dismissed the guards and then said to Captain Rainer, "Sit." He watched her for a minute just taking her in. After a long time of them just looking at each other he spoke, "I am going to send half of you back to Earth as long as you promise not to engage in this war anymore."

"Only half?"

"The other half will be sent to the Alliance," he was watching her reaction. He wondered if the rumors about the Alliance's demographic problems had reached human ears.

Kara was trying to figure out why he wouldn't send them all home. "What could you possibly want with only half of us?"

"Human women are considered Alliance citizens now, so it is our responsibility to keep you safe. You and your female crew will be sent to our capital planet."

Kara looked at him in disbelief, "Admiral, I believe there's been a mistake. We are human and nothing more."

Tir looked into her big brown eyes and shook his head, "No Captain, you are Alliance citizens now and that comes before your humanity. Forget being human."

Kara stood up, she was angry. She reached for where her gun would normally be and realized that she did not have it.

He moved quickly and had his sword at her throat in seconds. He had no intention of really hurting her, but just wanted to prove a point. "Captain, your dying will not change the facts. Neither you nor I made this law, but it is the law, and human women are ours now." Tir loved the way she smelled. He wanted to hold her this close again, but not like this.

"It sounds like you need me more than I need you, so I doubt you'll kill me," she tried to punch him and get away, but he just held her more tightly against him. She could not help but notice how hard his body felt against hers and wondered if he was just born pure muscle.

He grabbed her even more tightly and forced her back down into the chair. Still holding her, he activated the chair's restraints on her wrists and ankles then sat down himself across from her. He was amused watching her struggle. He said nothing and just patiently waited for her to calm down all the while thinking about how she might be in bed. He could not help it. His mind raced through different scenarios of foreplay. He figured that she would be feisty, and he had to admit to himself that he found that arousing.

When she finally stopped struggling, he said, "I will have the men from your crew sent back to Earth or I can simply execute them now if you do not cooperate." He was speaking to her casually, "The choice is yours."

"I must warn you, we would rather die than be sex slaves, Admiral. We will not last long in captivity." Everyone in the galaxy knew that the Alliance kept slaves.

"Captain, we are not savages. You and your female crew will be wives and have a better life than you would have ever had on Earth. You should be thanking me." He had never been to Earth, but he knew they were thousands of years behind the Alliance in terms of quality of life and technology.

"Why would the most racist and most powerful civilization in the galaxy suddenly want human women for wives?" He did not answer her but just waited for her to figure out. After a couple of minutes, she continued, "Oh I see, something is wrong with your women and now you think you can just take from us? That is not how it works. I am sure the Galaxy Court will have something to say about this. You cannot just pillage a civilization. And what is to say whatever is affecting your women will not kill us too?"

"We are the Alliance, we absolutely can just take human women. Do you think the Galaxy Court is going to care what happens to humans? You are nothing. They will probably congratulate us for bringing you out of the dark ages even if we are taking a risk that whatever is affecting our women will affect you too. Again, you should be thanking me Captain. You will be one of the lucky ones as we are only going to take two billion human women to begin integration." Earth's population was 13 billion. The Alliance population was well over two-hundred billion.

"Take that little sword then and kill me. I will not marry one of you. I will not participate in such a barbaric practice." Earth might have been behind the entire galaxy militarily speaking but humans considered themselves to be quite sophisticated culturally and had given up religion and marriage centuries ago.

He could not help but smile at her then. He loved her fierceness and he reminded himself, she was the one who lured and beat Alliance ships, she was courageous and smart. "I admire your spirit Captain, so I have decided to make an example of you. You will be the first to marry, here onboard my ship tonight and if you resist, I will execute every male from your crew until you agree," he was willing to just execute all the human men anyway, all except their doctor who might be useful.

"My crew would all rather die than see women barbarically married."

"Really? Why don't we put this to the test then," he could not tell if she was lying, so he ordered his guards to bring in two, human, male officers.

Her first and communication officers were brought in. The latter had tears in his young eyes and looked scared. She could tell that her first officer was ready to die, almost expected it, but in the end, she could not let them die over something so ridiculous. She could run away from a husband, they could not be raised from the dead. Then she began thinking maybe she could even steal some Alliance weapons and possibly a ship from whoever her husband was supposed to be.

Before the Admiral gave the order to execute her men she said, "I agree Admiral. I will marry. Let my men go."

Her first officer began to protest but was punched and subsequently led away with her communications officer by the same guards who brought them in.

Admiral Tir was pleased. He looked at her considering all the single men on his ship and who he would give her to. Any of his men would obey him and take her as a wife, but he decided in that moment, that he would take her as his own wife. If it did not work out, an unfortunate accident would befall her. He recalled the guards then and had them take her to his quarters.

Kara wondered if he was going to marry him herself. She hoped so. He was powerful, and she would have access to steal better weapons, secrets and credits from him, which would be useful for her escape, and afterwards, in case he would pursue her.

Admiral Tir summoned his junior lieutenant and ordered him to procure some Alliance dresses for Captain Rainer from the replicator and get her to shower. He would marry her tonight and as much as he wanted to unzip that filthy uniform and ravish her as an inferior human, he also wanted her as clean as possible too. As this was going to be their wedding night, he did not want her to hold this little thing over him, just in case this marriage did turn out well in the future. He assured himself that he would have time to roleplay later with her human uniform, as he had no intention of returning her to his capital planet anytime soon.

Kara was led to the Admiral's quarters, shown the bathroom and told to undress and shower by a young man. She refused of course. The young man took out his sword and they had a scuffle, but in the end, her exhaustion and lack of food betrayed her, and he forced her into the shower by sword point.

When Kara entered the shower, it spoke to her and she jumped. She hated cleansing technology.

"Please state your name human," the shower ordered.

"Kara," she replied.

"Scanning. Be warned, the water temperature maximum is 25C."

The shower began raining down on her and she screamed as it was cold. The air was cold, and the water was cold.

The young man came inside the bathroom quickly to make

sure she had not hurt herself and she told him sternly, "Get out." Then she stood still and let the cold water run over her, trying not to shiver. She had some cuts from her scuffle with the young man which stung when the shower provided her with soap and shampoo, but she had to admit to herself it was good to get clean and the soap did smell rather nice even if she was freezing. Her nipples stiffened partly from the cold and partly from thinking about the Admiral. It had been so long since was with a man and this alien was strangely attractive.

When the water stopped the shower dried her off with some waves of wind from top and bottom. Then she looked in the mirror over the sink and was offered a hand-held laser to brush her teeth. She used it. She suspected it was the Admiral's, so she felt some retribution in using his laser tooth brush.

She walked into the bedroom naked, but clean and dry. She had expected to see the young man there, but she was alone. She took in the Admiral's quarters, he had three rooms, a bedroom, a sitting area and a dining room. She thought to herself, *Well, being an Admiral in the Alliance certainly has its benefits*. She opened his wardrobe, inside hung three black uniforms. She saw some boxes stacked under them and was about to go through them when the young man returned.

He set three, typically plain, Alliance dresses out for her on the bed. They had no patterns and she knew from seeing them before that they would drape unattractively, like soft boxes, over her body. She reflected that Alliance women had very little in the way of curves on their bodies so maybe that was a reason they liked the boxy look. She did not want to wear one of these ugly dresses.

"Where is my uniform?"

"I threw it in the recycling," he lied, Admiral Tir told him to keep it and try to clean it. "Choose a dress. I made these based on your uniform measurements and I made them warm as you are human."

She just took the black dress, she was very cold without any clothes on, "Where are my undergarments?"

"Alliance women wear nothing but stockings under their dresses," he handed her some almost transparent stockings and then turned and put the other two dresses in the Admiral's wardrobe.

That's when it hit her, *He is marrying me himself.* Well, she had to give it to him, he would not ask anyone of his crew to do what he was not prepared to do himself and she thought, in a strange way, that was quite honorable of him. "Where are my shoes?"

"I did not have time to have any made. You will have some by tomorrow."

"I need some shoes now."

The young man shook his head, "Tonight you will marry. You will not be leaving these quarters for many days. Shoes are not a priority."

The young man watched her struggle with the clasps on the dress and finally just did them for her. The dress had clasps that became invisible all along the sides and she had to admit although the dress was unattractive it was both warm and surprisingly comfortable.

She sat on the sofa with the boy across from her for at least a while. They were not speaking. She had tried to ask him many questions to get any information she could that would help her escape, but he had been trained well. In the silence she nodded off to sleep. Soon her dreams drifted to a long-haired alien with a muscular body putting his hands and tongue all over her. She was awoken suddenly by the sound of the door opening and was wondering if she had made any sounds during her sleep. She felt her cheeks were flushed and she was soaking wet, but the young man's face expression was still very much neutral when she looked over.

When Admiral Tir came in, the young man bowed and left quickly. Kara stood up waiting for him to speak. He looked at her and then went into his bedroom to retrieve his comb and then handed it to her silently. She did not thank him but sat back down and began combing through her short hair which had some knots as it had dried badly with the shower dryer.

Tir watched her struggle with her hair for a couple minutes before he couldn't take it anymore. He silently took the comb from her hand, sat next to her on the sofa and said, "Just relax" then he combed her hair slowly and gently until there were no more knots. If he was going to marry this human, he wanted her relaxed and not looking like an ungroomed garden animal. And if he was being honest with himself, he had wanted to run his hands through her brown hair since he met her, and he was not disappointed. Her hair was soft and light. He purposely touched the back of her neck gently with his hand, with every stroke of the comb. He was pleased that she did not tell him to stop or move away from him. It was apparent that she enjoyed his touch which was good because soon he would be touching her everywhere, inside and out.

She was surprised by his gentleness. She found that she was becoming aroused by his actions, his closeness, the smell of him, like petrichor, and the power he had over her. She turned to look around at him when he had finished, and their eyes met. *Are you not going to kiss me? Do aliens kiss?*

He was amused by her face expressions. First, it was obvious that she wanted some more physical attention but then her expression changed, and it became apparent something completely different had crossed her mind. He caressed her cheek with the back of his hand and got up to return the comb to its place in the bathroom. When he returned to the sitting room, he found her in front of the locked door. He came up strongly and silently behind her and unlocked the door and opened it in front of her. His body was pressed up against hers. She didn't move but just looked in front of her. His guards were there, they looked at him. He nodded, then he closed the door again and locked it. She still didn't move.

He bent down, put his hands on her shoulders and whispered in her ear, "You can't leave, we will marry, and you are still my prisoner, until you prove yourself."

His breath on her ear sent shivers through her body, she could not think for a minute.

Before she could say anything, he guided her back to the sofa. "Have a seat."

She did. She watched him go into his dining room and pour himself a cup of wine. She admired his muscular figure, his jewelry no doubt won for bravery and battles won. She wondered how old he was then. Older than her, but it was so difficult to know with aliens. She was too tired to ask, young enough to still not be married she told herself, but then wondered if he had a past wife who had died. "Have you been married before?"

Tir thought this was a strange question, "No, why would you ask that?"

"What do I know about marriage? How old you are?"

"How old do I look to you?" he asked, wondering for the first time if she found him as attractive as he found her.

Kara got up from the sofa and stood right in front of him. She touched his face. He had few wrinkles and his skin was still quite taunt. She knew Alliance citizens lived to be about 300 years, so she said, "I would guess you to be about 50 years old."

He smiled, "No too far off. I am forty-five."

"Young to be an admiral," she commented wondering how he rose to such a high position so quickly.

"As you are young to be a captain, Kara."

Kara's body resonated when he used her given name. "How do you know how old I am?"

"You forget, your ship is docked her. I have looked through all your files and many of your personal logs while you were getting cleaned up."

She said nothing.

He touched her hair, "You are nothing short of impressive."

"And you are not worried I will kill you in your sleep? As you said, I am still your prisoner and the war is still going on."

"It is a chance I am willing to take," he took a sip of wine and then she took the glass out of his hands and finished it all.

He poured himself another glass of wine just watching her

walk back to the sofa. He thought she still looked beautiful even out of her uniform although he could no longer see the swell of her breasts or hips. He was looking forward to running his hands all over her soft and warm skin, to see all her skin color variations and to taste all of her.

Kara realized that they were probably waiting for something or someone to get this marriage thing over. Or maybe they were just waiting for him to have some wine, she had no idea. She closed her eyes and tried to concentrate on making a plan. Now all she wanted was sex, food, sleep and then escape, in that order.

As the minutes passed, she tried to remember what she knew about Alliance men. She knew that they were rumored to be attentive lovers and brave soldiers but not much else. She knew that the Alliance was a matriarchal society. She hoped that that would be helpful in her escape, but then she opened her eyes and looked at him and thought, *But that also makes him a bit of my responsibility too and he saved my and my crew's lives*.

The door chimed. His chief medical officer came in. Tir spoke to him quietly, she didn't care to listen. Tir held out a glass of wine for his doctor. Siu took the wine and they both looked at Kara.

Siu needed this glass of wine as much as Tir did. He and Tir, of course, had shared women before, they had been friends a long time, but this was different, it was marriage, there would be no sharing with his wife and she was human. Neither one of them had ever seen a human before, she was gorgeous and so curvy. Siu was jealous of Tir and would have to refrain himself from joining in as he was supposed to be the witness to the consummation of their marriage not an active participant.

After ten minutes Tir asked, "Kara are you ready?"

She didn't answer.

He walked over and stood in front of her and repeated himself, forcing her to look up and stand up in front of him by putting both hands gently on either side of her face.

His hands were cool and his rings cold. Quickly her mind

raced to where those hands and rings would be on her body soon. Her body wanted him without question, "Ready Admiral." She thought of her lack of underwear and wondered if they waited any longer if her wetness would start to run down the top of her thighs and soak the stockings when she stood up.

He urged her to her feet and then let go of her, "You will be one of the few who calls me by my given name now Tir."

"Tir," when she said his name, something resounded through them both as if it felt so right and she had said it before a million times.

Tir knew what it meant. They were destined for each other and perhaps in another timeline they were already together. He instinctively reached out a hand to touch her cheek.

"Is there some Alliance magic at work here?" she asked quietly.

"This is what destiny feels like."

"I don't believe in destiny, another archaic belief."

Their eyes were still holding, and he kissed her passionately. She was so warm. His tongue was tasting her, and she was so human, so sweet and so warm. He was exploring her and with each new sensation he was intrigued by her alienness and wanted more. After a few minutes, he pulled away, he realized they needed to say some words to be married. He had to give her his necklace. Then after the words were spoken, he was going to have every inch of her and give every inch of himself to her.

Siu watched them and thought, *It's been a long time since I've seen such attraction especially in a married couple.* While Tir went to retrieve the marriage necklace, Siu poured himself another large glass of wine.

Tir returned with the necklace in hand and then led Kara into the bedroom. He turned her around and placed the necklace on her. It was heavy, large and colorful, "Kara Rainer of Earth, I pledge myself to you in wedlock." He turned her back around, "Now you say it Kara."

"Tir, I don't know if you have another name, from the Alliance, I pledge myself to you in wedlock." She could not help but put her hand on the necklace. "What is this?"

"It is a marriage necklace. Do not take it off."

Kara looked over at the doctor, "Is he going to watch?"

"We must have a witness," Tir replied casually wanting nothing more now than to consummate this marriage.

"Seriously?"

"Yes," Tir took both her hands and kissed her for a long time, allowing her time to relax. After several minutes, he slowly let go of her hands and began exploring her body. He was touching her everywhere over the fabric of her dress. He loved lingering in the excitement of what was to be. Caressing her nipples through the fabric of her dress and bringing his hands up the full-length of her stockings and then just brushing around the tops of her thighs where the stockings stopped. He could feel her wet arousal on the top of her thighs and it made him want her even more.

He was undressing her slowly now. He began with the top of the dress, pulling it down slowly, exposing the tops of her shoulders and his lips were everywhere. She tried to close her eyes, but she kept looking at his doctor who was watching them. She could not decide if this was completely barbaric or sexy. She wondered if he was going to join in too or just watch. She lost her train of thought then and closed her eyes with pleasure when Tir reached her breasts and said sweetly, "Pink," then sucked and caressed them equally his tongue and fingers.

Tir had never seen such perfect breasts in his entire life. They fit neatly into his hands and were soft mounds with pink nipples, just like the color of her lips. He loved stroking them and drawing on them with his mouth, and even more, the small, gratifying sounds she was making when he touched them. He was grateful he had not given her to anyone else on the ship.

After about ten minutes, he pulled her dress further down revealing the top of her hips. He gently kissed all around her flat stomach and ran his hands along the curve of her hips, enjoying the floral taste of her mixed with something else, he could not identify, but found exotic and erotic. Then he drew her dress down further to reveal her vulva and was surprised to see a small amount of brown hair there. He immediately reveled in the strong scent of her. He guided her to lay back on the bed and began kissing around the patch of hair, gently stroking her vulva, hoping that just as with Alliance women, that there would be a clitoris there to make her orgasm.

It had been a long time since Kara had been with a man who knew what he was doing. Most men had no idea about women's bodies and just went in for a good rut and unfortunately most human women allowed it. Now she thought, *It is ironic that here I am with an alien who cares more about my sexual pleasure than most human men.* She was so close to coming now and it had only been minutes. He had not even touched her clitoris yet.

Tir looked to his doctor across the room as to ask with his eyes, 'Do human women have a clitoris?'

Siu nodded and then Tir continued what he was doing. It was not long before he saw Kara's body opening to him. She was so beautiful and pink. It was not long before he replaced his fingers caressing her vulva and thighs lightly with his tongue. He licked her lightly everywhere before finally settling on her clitoris. He had not expected her to almost come so quickly. Siu would think he was rushing the sex if he made her come right away. So, he backed off then and moved his mouth and hands back to her breasts. She did not like that at all though and began wrapping her legs around him trying to get herself off on his clothed body. He put his hands on her hips and pushed her down. He hovered over her and said, "Kara, open your eyes," she did. Her pupils where huge with desire and it pleased him, "We are not nearly done here, I promise."

Kara was looking at this gorgeous alien through a cloudy, lustful haze wondering, *Yes, but I can come more than once.* Her body was so on the edge, all she wanted to do was orgasm, but he was far away from her now and all she felt was cold air on her sex. He was sucking her nipples, but she desperately wanted him to touch her clitoris, to lick her until she was writhing in his mouth. She tried to move one of her hands to take care of it

17

herself, but he grabbed her hand and then put it with her other hand above her head and held them there with one of his hands while he continued to pleasantly torture her with kisses and caresses in all the wrong places.

Tir was pleased that she was so close that she was willing to just take matters into her own hands. After he was sure she would not orgasm immediately, he slowly returned to her clitoris, kissing her all along the way from her breasts, stomach, top and sides of her thighs. Then he began to build her back up only with his tongue.

Kara thought that she was in heaven, if she had believed in heaven. He was giving her so much pleasure with his tongue now she could not move. She just stayed as still as possible. She knew that in minutes he was going to make her orgasm harder than any other man before him and in less time as well.

Then he stopped.

She did nothing for a minute. Then she said, "Don't stop," and put her hands on his head.

"Don't stop, what?" he was looking up at her expectantly. He was confident he would be able to bring her back to come so hard in a few minutes, he wanted to play with her a bit.

She was thinking, but all she could think about was her pleasure. "Don't stop, Admiral?" she hazarded.

He didn't move.

She tried to shimmy her body closer to his face. He held her thighs tightly to keep her still.

"Don't stop," she began and then was thinking and then almost screamed it when she realized what he wanted, "husband."

He rewarded her by going back to her with his tongue and working her up again. This time she could not help but move a bit. She wanted this so badly. He began putting a finger into her vagina and she moaned. She really thought she was going to die of pleasure now.

She repeated the forbidden word to him a couple times more to make sure he would not stop again, "Husband...husband..." then it was just all sounds of building pleasure.

"You are so tight Kara," he had heard that human men had smaller penises, but he had not really considered what they might mean for human women until now. She was warm, wet and tight, and it made him even more aroused when he thought how that was going to feel around his penis.

He was licking and moving his finger in and out of her rhythmically. She was so wet she could feel her moisture against the top of her thighs. She was in ecstasy. She had no idea how long this went on for but when he finally brought her to orgasm it lasted for at least a minute or two and it took her some more minutes to recover herself. Then she began trying to take his clothes off, but completely unfamiliar with the Alliance clasps she finally gave up and admitted, "I've no idea how to take off your clothes."

He watched her trying to figure out the clasps on his clothing and thought that humans might really be the most adorable species in the galaxy. When she finally gave up, he showed her how they easily came undone by applying pressure on the inside of the clasp. She was undressing him now and touching his body with her warm hands. He was watching those hands, marveling at the diversity in color, her golden hands on his grey skin.

She managed to take all his clothing off and marveled at his muscular body with no hair anywhere. She immediately went down to her knees to take his large, ridged penis in her mouth. He realized what she was going to do then and said, "No," he said sternly. He wanted to explain that it went against the goddess unless she was with child but couldn't in the moment. He just took her hand and urged her up and back to the bed.

"I want to be on top," she wanted to be more of an active participant. He was surprised but acquiesced to her request. He laid down and she positioned herself dripping wet over him. She began slowly taking him into her. "You are so big and the ridges..." she trailed off. He felt so good inside of her she could not speak anymore, but she did remember the doctor was still there and made eye contact with him as she lowered herself onto Tir. It felt sexy that he was watching her. She wondered if he would masturbate thinking about her later and that also gave her pleasure.

Tir was watching her and thought she looked like the embodiment of the goddess herself as she slowly lowered herself onto his penis. The marriage necklace was nestled divinely between her breasts that jiggled with her movements. Up and down. She was so tight, wet and warm it took everything he had not to orgasm immediately. He was surprised by her comment then and had to ask through the sex haze, "Human men don't have ridges on their penises?"

She was beyond talking.

He grabbed her hips tightly to stop her from moving and said, "Kara, open your eyes and answer the question."

Kara was shocked he stopped her. She opened her eyes, "Just smooth, now let's get back to this. I don't want your doctor to think I'm a terrible lover." She looked up at the doctor again. She could see desire in his eyes too. She looked back down at Tir then and began moving watching him watching her. Watching his hands move over her hips and breasts.

He let her ride him faster and faster, even though he knew he was flirting with his own end. He put his hands on her breasts. He loved watching them sway with her movements and being able to hold them and make her moan a bit.

"Put your hands on my hips," she said breathlessly. He did and then she said, "Press me down harder against you."

Tir had his hands on her hips pressing he down in circular motions, so she could grind against him. Then he urged her up and stopped her. "Let me lead you," then he went slowly up and down so the tip of his penis would gently touch her.

"That feels so good," she said quietly. "I am going to come again, but I want to come with your penis inside of me."

He guided her hips down on top of him so that his penis was fully inside of her again and she began grinding. He put his hands on her hips again and moved one finger closer to her anus, he was flirting with it there to see her reaction. He finally gently stuck it in and saw her pleasure. He put his other hand between them to make sure that her clitoris was rubbing against his thumb while she moved on top of him. It was not long before she was coming again. He had to really control himself not to come himself.

As soon as she finished, he gently flipped her onto her back and said, "You are so beautiful wife. I am going to enjoy having sex with you every day." Then he found her vagina and entered her again. The new position added new friction.

Kara was looking up at this gorgeous strong grey man who was now pounding into her and thinking that maybe being married would not be that bad. She lifted her legs so high that it was obvious she wanted him to take them over his shoulders.

Tir held her ankles together over one of his shoulders has he pounded into her. He loved the way her breasts moved with each thrust. He would have her again and again like this. It was not long before he lost himself in all the warm, wet exoticness of his human. Then he laid down next to her and pulled her close.

After a minute Siu rose and said, "May the gods be with you both and grant you many daughters." The doctor then let himself out.

Kara laughed, "I forgot that he was here."

"No, you didn't. I saw you looking at him every once and awhile."

"It was shocking to have an audience."

"Did you find it arousing?"

Kara had no reason to lie, "Yes."

"I am sure he did too. You are gorgeous Kara and you put on quite a show." He absently was rubbing the exotic hair on her vulva as they talked.

"What do you mean?"

"Human women are much more vocal than Alliance women, all your wonderful sounds. I am sure that the doctor has gone to relieve himself with another woman onboard, but he will only be disappointed she is not human."

"You have other women onboard? I thought there were only men on Alliance ships."

"Of course, there are women," he did not want to mention what kind of women they might be.

She did not say anything for many minutes until Kara broke the silence, "Are we married now?"

"Yes," he said without looking at her and thinking how strange it was he finally had a wife and a human wife at that.

"What do you expect me to do as a wife?"

Tir had never heard such a ridiculous question. "We will have children together in a monogamous relationship. The Alliance needs female children."

"Is that it? How do you know we can have children together?"

"We know," he assured her.

"I'm not like a pet or anything. What am I bound by?"

"You are bound by your loyalty to me and I to you. You're not a pet."

"Can I leave your quarters?"

"Not until you prove your loyalty. But I'll allow you to see your crew off and tell your women what is happening under the supervision of my guards. If you try to escape you will be punished."

"How do Alliance husbands punish their wives?"

Tir sat up and looked down at her in all astonishment, "Do you want me to punish you right, now just for asking?"

Kara looked at him and was ready for him to take her again in all new ways. She wanted to see his dominant side, "Feed me and then punish me for asking husband."

DEPARTURES

Human Captain Kara Rainer and Alliance Admiral Tir had been married for approximately one hour. They had just consummated their marriage under the watchful eye of chief medical officer Doctor Siu. Kara was lying on the bed naked. She touched the heavy and ornate necklace the Admiral had given her, "Do your people always give necklaces away when they marry?"

Tir shifted in the bed so he could look at her. He ran a finger down the side of her cheek, down her neck and stopped at the necklace, admiring it against her golden skin. "No, we usually exchange bracelets but I have none here. But we do give jewelry to our wives as presents the day after we marry, so I thought this would do for now."

"Are the bracelets like shackles?"

He frowned and looked into her eyes, "I know you think I have forced you, but this is meant to be."

"You forced me to marry you, that is true," she ran a hand down his strong grey chest. "I don't understand why we needed to be married."

"As I have told you we have…"

"I know, a demographics problem, you need women, but we don't need to be married to do this," she moved her hand lower to stroke his penis and he closed his eyes momentarily. "Not that I didn't enjoy the little show we put on, I've never done that before, or sleeping with an alien, I just don't understand this need to say we belong to each other. It is so archaic and you know, of course you know, I will try and escape any chance I get."

He removed her hand from his penis and pushed her on her back, holding her hands above her head. His finger found her vagina and he entered her, all the while looking down at her. "Open your eyes," Kara could hardly obey him as he was giving her so much pleasure, "This is your new life. You are an Alliance citizen and that becomes before everything you knew before. Moreover, you are mine and I am yours. If you try and escape you will be punished. If you manage to escape and I retrieve you, I will kill you myself."

She wanted to protest but he was thrusting into her with his ridged penis in such a way she didn't care if he kept her chained to his bed now forever as he felt so good.

"Do you hear me?" he said a bit breathlessly.

She nodded and then he let go of her hands and grabbed her hips to thrust into her more deeply. She was lost in ecstasy.

An hour later, Kara lay across Tir's strong, grey, naked body, "Tell me again, what are the differences between humans and Alliance citizens?"

He answered her quietly while running his hand through her brown hair absently, "We all have grey skin and black hair and green or grey eyes. We are not as colorful or as beautiful as humans. And as you noticed, ridges in certain intimate places."

She smiled and put her hand down to feel the ridges on his penis, but they were only noticeable to the touch and not protruding against his skin as they did when he was aroused. She wondered why human men had not developed such a wonderful enhancement, given the two species were almost identical. "But there must be more differences?"

"Well, there is the heat, we are comfortable at 15C whereas I think you like it at 19C?"

"Try 23C, but it is not like I am going to die at 15C, I just need warmer clothes."

Kara got up and went into the bathroom, then she came

back out and admitted, "I don't know how to work your toilet."

He got up and joined her in the bathroom. He could not help but touch her arm gently as he passed her. He loved the way she looked wearing the large, colorful necklace he had given her with no clothes on. It hung beautifully between her breasts as she stood waiting for him. He entered the bathroom and touched a section behind the toilet on the wall and a virtual menu appeared.

"I can't read Alliance," she said. "Human translators are for the spoken word only. Maybe you could get me an Alliance translator? Then, I could speak and read with everyone in the galaxy."

"Not until you have proven yourself loyal to the Alliance and me, until then I don't want you having access to everything in my quarters, so you will just have to memorize the basics." He then showed her which buttons to press. "The toilet will remember you after this." Then he left the bathroom and closed the door to give her some privacy.

Kara sat down on the toilet that now adjusted itself for her height and thought about her situation. She decided she would turn her translator on and off when she could, to try and learn not only their written language but their spoken language as well. She figured it could not be too difficult as she spoke a few Earth languages and she was surrounded by the Alliance language everywhere onboard his ship. Moreover, it would be a key to her escape. Humans still loved their little nuances so unlike the rest of the galaxy where every civilization had one language, humans still had many, so their translators could be mentally turned on and off. It was also true that humans took the time to learn other world's languages as well, something that aliens found useless and a waste of time. Kara smiled to herself, *Not such a waste of time now as she knew how to learn a foreign language, how to look for the patterns and practice.*

Kara now focused on the task at hand. It took her some time to relax and pee. She took in her physical self as she sat on the toilet. Her vagina felt it had been well-used by his large penis, her nipples raw from all the attention they had just received and she was somewhat shaky from all the orgasms, but surprisingly, she was still aroused. She still wanted him. After the toilet cleaned her, which was probably the most embarrassing part about smart toilets, she got up and looked at herself in the mirror.

The mirror greeted her which she also disliked, "Good evening Kara. You are lacking nutrition and are dehydrated. I recommend some food and water."

"I know," she answered the mirror back, "Tell me something useful, mirror."

"You have Admiral Tir's semen inside of you," said the mirror in a matter of fact tone.

"How do you know that?" She could not believe she was talking with the mirror, but she was too curious to just walk away.

"Your urine. You just used the toilet," answered the mirror.

"Stop talking to me," Kara half-whispered as she turned on the tap and splashed her face with some ice cold water.

"Would you like the water temperature warmer, Kara? It is set for Admiral Tir now."

"No, stop. Turn off. I don't want to talk to you mirror."

Tir heard Kara's conversation with the mirror and thought, *Humans really are the most adorable creatures in the galaxy.*

When she came out of the bathroom, she looked at Tir naked on the bed. He looked so good, long, strong and muscular. His ridged penis was resting but she knew she could get it to come alive again. Her mind raced to all the things she could do now, but then a hunger pang struck. "I have hardly eaten all week. I would love some food."

"We have missed the evening meal," admitted Tir.

"So?" she said not understanding the Alliance's strict cultural customs.

"We cannot eat when it is not meal time, it goes against the gods."

"I am human. I am hungry, and I don't believe in the gods,"

she realized by his stoic face expression that these lines were getting her nowhere. She tried again, "I cannot get pregnant if my body thinks I am starving. My crew and I have been on low-rations for weeks. I guarantee you, my body thinks I am starving."

He looked her over and thought that was probably not true as his doctor would have seen to that, but if she was hungry he would allow her some food, just to be hospitable. He reminded himself that she only arrived on the ship that morning and she probably had only had one meal today, if that. "What would you like to eat?"

"Vegetables, bread. Humans do not eat meat." She almost smiled thinking how easy that was to convince him to break some rules but was also concerned with how he just wanted to use her as a breeder, but then she wondered, *How strict are the rules about eating? Who knows? I should not congratulate myself too quickly.*

"Meat is good for you and it is what we have a lot of," he explained as he contacted his junior lieutenant on his communicator.

"It will make me ill and I will not eat it."

Tir looked at her and remembered his doctor's words, 'Make her as comfortable as possible.' So, he acquiesced to her request with a nod.

When the young man arrived, Tir left the bedroom naked to speak to him in the sitting room. Kara smiled to herself at this behavior, *Well, I guess you can just be naked and do what you need to do onboard an Alliance starship.*

When Tir returned he found Kara under the covers in his bed. "Are you cold?"

"How about we turn up the heat to 23C and I ask you if you are warm?"

He liked her sass, "Get up and put on your dress. Your food will be here shortly."

She got out of bed and tried to put on the plain, black Alliance dress again. Again, she struggled to get the clasps to close.

She knew how to open them from taking off his clothing, but his junior lieutenant had closed hers when she had put on this dress hours before.

Tir watched her struggle for a minute and then moved to show her how to close the clasps without speaking. Their fingers touched. She looked up at him as he finished, she ran her fingers through his hair to bring him closer for a kiss. Even though, this was a forced marriage she inexplicitly still found him irresistible. She whispered in his ear, "I just can't help myself when you are this close," and then sucked on his earlobe.

Tir made a pleasurable sound and began taking off the dress he just finished putting on her. His hands were on her firm breasts, licking and pinching her nipples. "I have never seen such perfect breasts," he said as he could not resist gently kneading them and watching them go taunt under his touch. Then he began making his way down her body, slowly kissing her, and licking her, "And your skin is so soft," his hands were on her hips now pulling the dress down to take it all the way off. "And I love this hair," he said looking up at her while he softly rubbed her vulva. He breathed her scent in then, "The exotic smell of you. Gods, I want to make you come from the touch of my tongue again."

"I am all yours, Admiral," she said with her head back, not realizing her mistake until he stopped touching her.

He could not believe she had just called him by his title. He looked up at her and realized then that she was enjoying herself so much that that was probably why she forgot. He still took his right hand and smacked her hard across the bottom though.

"Oww," she said and looked down at him questioningly even though she had really liked the tingling sensations on her skin where he had smacked her rear.

"Who am I to you?" She recognized his commanding voice and wondered if he spoke to his subordinates like this.

"Husband," she corrected herself, but then could not help but add the word, "Admiral," afterwards and he gave her a small smile and then smacked her rear again, this time on the other cheek.

"Who am I to you?" He was looking up at her, he was on his knees, so close to her that his lips were only millimeters away from touching her nether hair.

Kara knelt, to be on the same level as he was and kissed him passionately again. She was thrusting her hot tongue into his mouth and her hands were in his hair, pulling him towards her and holding him as steady as she could. In between kisses, she murmured the forbidden word, "Husband." She kissed his neck, "Husband," licked around his ear, "Husband," and sucked on his right nipple, "Husband." Her hand was on his ridged erect penis now and she was stroking it back and forth. "I want this inside of me again."

He pushed her on her back on the cold floor and moved down her body with more kisses. Everywhere he left a kiss was followed by her skin feeling the cold and it was making her even more aroused. By the time he was stroking her vulva and the top of her thighs, she was begging for him to make her come. "Please."

He looked up at her, his green eyes filled with amusement and desire, "Please what?"

"Please make me come Husband. I love the way you lick me." He then began licking her clitoris and she stayed so still, it felt so good. She did not want to move in case she broke the trance. After a couple minutes, a huge wave of pleasure over-took her.

He was tightly holding her thighs so that she would not move away when the orgasm began to hit her. He had never been with a woman who was so responsive to his touch and he thought again, *It is because we are destined to be together.* But just because they were destined, he was under no illusion that it would always be so easy. The gods of course would make it this easy to begin with but then make things more complicated. It was blasphemy to think they did it for the gods' own pleasure but sometimes he really believed that they did.

After she had recovered herself, she tried to go down on him, but he would not allow her. "Why not? Don't people in the Alliance suck penises?"

"Of course, we do, but it is forbidden unless you are with child." He left off the other part, 'or another man or slave'. He knew, no one in the galaxy liked to talk about Alliance slaves.

"Not even if you don't come?"

"There is always some before so, no." He flipped her onto her stomach then and pulled her up towards him and said casually, "But I have no doubt you will become pregnant soon and it makes me so aroused thinking about your mouth sucking me off." He positioned her with his hands on her hips.

He entered her so strongly and quickly from behind it took her breath away. His large, erect penis with its ridges were hitting all the right spots inside of her vagina. He was filling her completely and she loved it, this rougher sex. She gasped with pleasure and forgot to comment that she was on birth control, so she was probably not going to get pregnant anytime soon. As he was pounding into her, she vaguely thought it was probably a good thing to keep that information to herself until she could gauge the whole situation and just enjoy the sex with this man.

His hands were on the curve of her hips as he strongly thrust in and out of her. He loved the feel of her tight, wet vagina taking the entire length of his penis like this. She was making the sexiest little pleasurable sounds. The only thing he didn't like is that he could not see her breasts moving with their movements.

He tried to urge her onto her back, "No, don't move. This feels so good. I want you to take me like this, faster Tir. Faster." She loved the feel of him and she thought, *For the first time in my life a man might make me orgasm while having sex.* She was urging him on and then it happened. She came again without and any more clitoral stimulation and she thought, *We will have sex every day before I try to escape.*

He came then shortly after. Tir was unaware of how good she found their love making. For him, of course he was enjoying himself, being with such a responsive and exotic human woman, it was something he had never done before, but making a woman orgasm many times during sex was normal for him. Alliance women expected it and the men performed.

Both Kara and Tir were motionless for a half a minute, then he stood up and put his hands on her hips to help her up too. She looked up at him and said seriously, "Thank you for helping me with the clasps on my dress."

He smiled down at her, "The food is here. I heard him come in." He picked up the discarded black dress and began to dress her again.

Copious amounts of semen and her natural lubricant were running down her legs and into the stockings she was wearing, but she didn't care, she was starving. She figured everything she had on, including her body would need to be washed anyway. She walked out through the sitting room into the dining room where one plate of food was waiting. Alliance food was famous for being bland and terrible, so she did not expect much. She sat down in front of the food and began eating with the three-pronged fork that was left next to the plate. She thought to herself, *I love eating with a trident.*

He came in and sat across from her at the silver table.

"Are you going to watch me eat?"

"It is bad luck to eat alone," he explained pouring himself a cup of wine.

"So Tir, how religious would you say you are?" She was thinking to herself, *No fellacito, because it goes against the gods, no eating alone because no doubt this angered the gods too...*

"As religious as most Alliance citizens, I would say. Are you spiritual at all?"

"No," she answered evenly. Then she concentrated on eating the blandest food she had ever had in her life, but she didn't care because she realized now, that she was so hungry she might have eaten anything, even a piece of meat.

"Privately, your spiritual life is your own, but publically as my wife, you must abide by Alliance religious traditions."

"Or else you will punish me?" she looked into his eyes with

both desire and a little humor.

"Yes," he said calmly. His mind then rushed to all the ways he would like to punish her and then his mind rested on one particular punishment he would subject her to when she was done eating.

She took the wine jug and poured herself some wine to help combat the blandness of the food. "What happens now?"

"What do you mean?"

"We are married and then what? Will I live here with you?"

"For the time being I will keep you here with me. As long as the war is going on, I can justify your presence by saying that you are providing useful information against the Jahay. Which, by the way, I expect you to do, not that I think they would share much with a human."

She dismissed his prejudiced comment, "Great," she said sarcastically, "I have always wanted to be seen as a traitor to my own people. Thank you."

He frowned at her, "Being my wife is a gift Kara. You are an Alliance citizen now."

She wanted to roll her eyes but resisted. She reminded herself, *Keep him happy so he trusts you and you can run away with technology, credits, weapons and a ship.* "You keep saying that, and I will admit you saved my crew's lives and my own and of course, it goes without saying, that the sex is amazing, but other than that, you are still humans' enemy in the current war and now I have lost my ship and my position in the human fleet all for what? Good sex?"

"Once you have proven your loyalty to me and the Alliance, I will give you a ship in my fleet," he said seriously. "Earth will become a vassal to the Alliance and we will need to protect you with a human fleet. It would be a waste if you didn't get a command again, you are too good of a strategist and a leader to do anything else."

She tried not to be charmed by his compliments, but she could not help it. He was an Admiral in the Alliance, they were the most powerful and feared species in the galaxy and she doubted he got to this position by his good-looks alone. "You mean you need a fleet to protect human women in our little corner of the galaxy before anyone notices that we are yours now and sees an opportunity to hit you where it hurts the most."

"More or less. Don't look as if this is the worst thing that could ever happen. You could be dead. Humans could be our slaves or slaves to the Jahay. Neither of those things will happen now."

"Why didn't you just ask humans to consider helping you with this demographics issue before this war started with the Jahay?"

"We did not want to waste our time if you said 'no' and to be honest I do not think the pride of the High Council could take it if humans, the most technologically unevolved civilization in the galaxy, denied us."

"Charming," she said sarcastically.

"I will not mince words with you Kara. And you can't tell me that you are unaware of your species' status in the galaxy."

She wanted to change the subject back to her getting her own ship, "When I have proven my loyalty to you, which won't take long, will I get my own ship again? Will you give me the *Dakota* or an Alliance ship? An Alpha ship?"

He laughed then, "Kara once you prove yourself and your loyalty, I will give you a Beta ship to begin with and if you are really good, I might even let you bring some of your crew along. As for the *Dakota* it belongs in a museum. By the way, tomorrow morning you will see your crew off and if you want to retrieve anything from your ship you should take it then. I will of course be sending your male crew back in the *Dakota*. Don't get any ideas though, you will be guarded the entire time."

"I still need shoes, your young man said he didn't have time when he gave me the dress and I have no idea where my other shoes are."

"We are still in the middle of a war and he had other things to attend to first. You will have some shoes by tomorrow."

"And I guess I don't need pajamas either," she said with a hint of a smile.

"We do not wear such things as they are unhealthy. Especially, if you are sleeping with your husband. Skin to skin contact is best for sleep and good health. I wonder what other kinds of human habits I will have to break you from?"

"I am going to miss pajamas in my new life," she said resentfully more to herself than him and then decided she would bring hers from her quarters on the *Dakota*. He would just have to deal with it. It was too cold in his quarters not to have pajamas.

She had finished eating, drank all the wine in her cup and then looked at him questioningly, "What should we do now? Are you very busy since, as you keep reminding me, as if I needed reminding, we are in the middle of a war? Or do you want to do some more sleeping with the enemy?"

"Kara you are no longer the enemy, you are my wife and an Alliance citizen, although I will admit still my prisoner as well until you recognize and start acting accordingly. As for my professional responsibilities, my first officer will contact me if there is an emergency. Otherwise I have tonight to spend with you and I believe your words before were, 'Feed me and then punish me for asking husband.' So now that I have fed you, we can move onto the punishment."

She smiled at him. She could see the desire in his eyes. She wondered then how many times a 45 year old Alliance man could have sex in a night. "I am impressed by your stamina."

He smiled at her then and it was the first time she had really seen him smile and he said, "It is only because I have such a beautiful specimen from a far corner of the galaxy before me." He stood up, "Come." He walked behind her with his hands lightly on her elbows, guiding her back into the bedroom. He left her standing in the center of the room while he went into his wardrobe and brought out some black ribbons. He gently took off her dress again, touching and kissing her body as he went. After some minutes, she stood in the center of the bedroom naked and she allowed him to tie her wrists together behind her back with one black ribbon and then he put the other ribbon over her eyes, so she was blinded. Then in quite a different tone of voice than before, he ordered her, "Don't move," and then she heard him walk out of the bedroom.

Kara was excited just standing there in the cold, being bound and naked, just waiting for him. Her nipples were stiff with excitement and cold and she could feel her sex becoming wet again in anticipation of what he was going to do to her.

Tir made her wait five minutes which he thought was long enough given that this was the first time they were doing this and that she was blindfolded. When he walked back into the room, he kneeled in front of her and ran is fingers lightly up her legs. When he reached her inner thighs he said, "So much wetness here. You must love my touch," he lightly was running is fingers over her inner thighs, the hair over her vulva and all the way back near her anus. He was mixing her wetness and his own semen. "My fingers, my tongue? Do you like the feel of my semen running down your legs?"

"Yes," she murmured.

He smacked her bottom hard.

She corrected herself, "Yes, Husband."

"Now, what was I punishing you for?"

"Asking about punishments," he smacked her again, "Husband." She had purposely forgotten that time and she thought, *Yes, spank me harder.*

"Asking about punishments. Usually, an Alliance man would never punish his wife, but you are human and must learn our ways, so I have no choice. I will punish you as I would a slave."

"A slave?"

He smacked her hard again.

"A slave, Husband?" she tried not to smile but couldn't help herself, so he smacked her again and that time really stung, but she was loving this.

"Yes, slaves brought to the capital usually have to be trained with rewards and punishments. I will do the same with you."

He was rubbing her rear, "Now your punishment for even asking about punishments will be 20 lashes with this little whip I have here. Put your hands out, palms up."

She did as he said and placed the whip in her hands, it felt firm, but soft.

"Feel the length of it Kara," he ordered her.

Her fingers ran along the whip that had two little tails. She was becoming so aroused thinking about him whipping her with this she inadvertently squeezed her thighs together in anticipation.

"I am going to whip you with this across your backside, thighs and vulva for asking. Twenty lashes."

"Yes Husband." *Do it*, she thought, *Oh yes, do it.*

"Lean forward to receive your punishment," he stood behind her still fully clothed, but completely aroused by the whole situation. He wished she would be a bit feistier, but he suspected that she was tired or that maybe she had never done this before and was unsure how to behave.

"Can I put my weight on the bed?"

There she was, his feisty captain, "No Wife. Bend over and keep your balance." He took the whip and struck her across her behind with it. "Count."

Kara bent over keeping her balance. The weight of her necklace felt like it kept her head parallel to the floor. She closed her eyes waiting for the first strike, "One, two three, four, five," he kept a slow and steady rhythm. On number five, he purposely struck her vagina then and she winced with both pleasure and pain.

"Did that feel good?" he was rubbing the whip up and down against the length of her vulva down to her vagina's entrance now. "You are so wet. I think you might be enjoying this too much. We should make it a bit more painful or you will not learn." He struck her then across the backside harder.

She winced but loved his strength, "Six, seven, eight, nine, ten." He was caressing her now, her breasts, her stomach, her neck, her hair. Then he grabbed her hair a little roughly and brought her close to him to whisper in her ear, which gave her shivers.

"Ten strokes left Wife, tell me where you want them." He pinched her nipples, "Here?" then his hand moved down to her vulva, and he stroked the long length of her, pulling a little at the hair there and she jumped at her sensitivity to his touch when he grazed her clitoris, "Or here?" He knelt then and began kissing her bottom that had turned so red. She jumped again from the warmth of his mouth and surprise of his actions. He held her thighs still as he continued to kiss her behind. He heard her moan a little. "Where do you want the last ten lashes Wife?" he said between kisses.

She was overwhelmed with cold and hot sensations. She wanted him to continue, she wanted him to lick her everywhere. She could hardly think and could not speak.

He kept kissing her, licking at her inner thighs from behind, "I am waiting."

"Here Husband," she said pointing to her vulva, "Do it here."

Tir looked up at her and smiled although she couldn't see it because she was blindfolded. He got to his feet and stood behind her. He guided her to lean back against his chest, he put one arm around her, his hand gripping one of her breasts, got a good angle and began.

She jumped when the first stroke hit her and forgot to count.

"Count," he ordered her quietly, pinching the nipple of the breast he held, his voice or his pinch, she could not decide which, sent a strong shiver through her body.

"Eleven, twelve, oh..." he rubbed the whip up and down touching her clitoris. She was so close to coming. "Thirteen, fourteen, fifteen..." he was rubbing her again and she was moving her hips to create even more friction. "Sixteen, seventeen, eighteen, nineteen, twenty." Then he moved away from her and just left her standing there alone in the middle of the room wanting. She heard him get on the bed. Kara suspected he was just watching her. She wanted him to come and finish this. To touch her. To do something. She wanted to take the blindfold off but couldn't because her hands were tied behind her. Now she began to struggle to get them out to get the blindfold off and or to bring herself to climax as she was so close it was almost painful.

"Don't struggle," he said from across the room. "Just wait."

"Wait for what… Husband?" she added it at the last minute to gain some favor.

"For me to decide how long we should punish you for."

She just stood there thinking, *I hope it won't be too long. I want him. I need him.*

Tir left her for ten minutes. He would have left her longer, but he realized how tired she was when she began to waver. He was impressed that she did not ask again to be released. He took off his clothes and guided her to the bed. "How do you want me to enter you?"

"Like a dog," she said breathlessly.

"What is a dog?"

She smiled, "Never mind, from behind, like before."

She got on her knees on the bed and he held her wrists with one hand and her hair with the other. Then he entered her and impaling her rhythmically with his penis. It seemed so primal as she was tied, blindfolded and he was holding her so tightly. He was controlling everything now and she screamed, "Yes, harder! Pull me against you harder."

He had never been with a woman that was so vocal, and he loved it. He grasped her wrists with strength he had never used with a woman before and increased his thrusts to be stronger and deeper. After a minute, he was rewarded by her coming again which easily brought on his own orgasm.

When she thought she would collapse out of pure exhaustion, he held her as he took off her blindfold and untied her wrists, but he noticed that she almost fell when he released her, so he easily picked her up into his arms and took her into the shower.

Tir looked down at Kara still in his arms and said, "This is probably going to be very cold for you." The water began to fall in that instant.

She screamed for how cold it was, it was not the 25C she thought was cold before, this was ice cold.

He set her down but held on to her, so she did not escape and suddenly the shower was providing soap and he was spreading it all around her body gently. He whispered in her ear, "I am sorry it is cold. This won't take long." After he washed her and himself quickly, the shower turned off, he grabbed his comb and combed her hair then his and then activated the dryer. Even though she was clean and dry now, she was still shivering. He picked her up again and carried her to the bed. He put her under the covers and said, "These blankets will adapt to the temperature you require so you will not be cold Kara. I will join you a minute. Try to warm up."

Kara nodded and then disappeared fully under the blankets. She was so cold she wanted her head and everything under them. It was not long before she began to warm up and she was relieved that he was right about the blankets.

When he came back to bed he got in and held up the blanket to look down at her, "Are you okay down there? Do I need to call the doctor?"

"I am getting warm," she said exhaustedly.

He moved down the bed, under the covers so that their heads were at the same level and their faces only inches apart. He stroked her brown hair, "Kara, we will try to come to some compromise about temperature."

She looked at him, into his green eyes and nodded. She had never been so intimate with a man she hardly knew before. She wondered if she would get to know him for better or worse by such close intimacy so soon. *Both,* she thought to herself and then wondered again, *How long will it take for him to trust me? A year? After some children?* She frowned and firmly ordered her mind to stop thinking and to work on warming her body, nothing more. She closed her eyes then and almost instantly drifted off into a deep sleep.

Tir watched Kara fall asleep as he stroked her hair. He felt this was so natural between them that he was convinced she had been sent to him by the gods. But he also reminded himself that even though they were obviously destined for each other, she still had a lot to learn and could not be trusted. Not until she at least bore him one child he decided.

His doctor had investigated all the information they had about human women and had briefed him before their wedding earlier this evening. Women from Earth ovulated more often than Alliance women and were fertile for less days per cycle, but Alliance men's sperm was stronger and would last longer. The doctor reckoned that he would be surprised if it took longer than two of Kara's cycles for her to become pregnant given her age and health. However, he did warn Tir that stress and lack of food could contribute to her not becoming pregnant. He was still stroking her hair even though he knew she was fully asleep and thought to himself, *You are strong and willing. We will have a daughter, it is the will of the gods.* Then he stopped stroking her hair, pulled her closely against him and brought both of their heads above the blanket.

Sometime during the night, Kara woke up and she was confused. She did not know where she was. She sat up.

Tir put a gentle hand on her arm and she instinctively swatted him away and tried to jump out of the bed.

"Lights on," Tir said and got out of bed to try and comfort Kara. She was looking at him confused, he wondered if she was still sleeping. "Kara? Kara?" She didn't answer him, so he tried to take her arm and she backed away. "Kara," he tried to grab her wrist again and succeeded. He held her close against him and stroked her hair. "You are safe," he said quietly a couple times to the top of her head. After about five or ten minutes, he could feel her begin to relax in his arms.

She had been so scared when she woke up and didn't know where she was and when the light was turned on, she was so confused. She had been dreaming and she was being interrogated by her own people for being a spy because of him. She kept saying that they weren't married, because in her mind she would never be married, she was human, but no one believed her. Kara breathed deeply, closed her eyes and tried to clear her head and think, everything had been so bizarre ever since she had said his name for the first time and it felt as if the galaxy had been turned upside down. She didn't believe in religion, fate or destiny, but she didn't know what to make of all of this and needed to ask a question that had been at the center of her dream, "Are you the Emperor?"

He stopped caressing her hair then and went still, "Why would you ask that?"

"I had a nightmare. I was being interrogated for being married to you by my own people and they said that you were the Emperor. I know that the Alliance has one, I just don't know who that is or how that works."

"I can assure you that I am not the Emperor," he said softly. He could feel her relax so he almost felt guilty, but he knew that the gods had sent her that dream to warn him to be honest with her, "But I am the successor." He could feel her stiffen again.

"What does that mean?"

"Successor?" He wondered if her translator was malfunctioning.

"No, I know what 'successor' means, but does that mean you will become Emperor tomorrow? Next year? What are you going to do with me when that happens? I know your people don't like aliens, will you discard me, kill me? Why did you marry me?" She was asking all the same questions now that she had been asked by both her interrogators and herself in her dream. She felt so weird, like different realities were colliding. She was herself, but not herself.

"It is five years before I am supposed to take over. And you are right, the Alliance would never stand for a human Empress, but when I saw you, I had to have you as my wife. Now I will probably abdicate, but that comes with its own issues."

"You don't have a brother or something to take it?" Although men and women had been equal on Earth for centuries, because the Alliance still practiced religion and marriage, she just assumed it was more like ancient Earth.

"It doesn't work like that, it is more based on merit not just birthright. People will be upset because they will feel I wasted their time and want to kill us for it. But if we take imperial power in five years they will be upset because you are human and want to kill us for that." Being Empress of the Alliance was one of the most important positions in the galaxy. They would be killed if he even attempted it with Kara, *Right now,* he thought, *But who knows what the next five years will bring. I cannot tell her yet though. She is far from ready.*

"Wow. When were you going to mention this?"

"I don't know? Perhaps after we were so in rapture with each other that you would not kill me for it." He touched her face lightly with the back of his thumb, "Please let's not think about this anymore. You are safe. I am never going to let you be imprisoned by your people. It was just a nightmare."

"Then why was some of it true?"

He shrugged, "The gods were trying to tell you something."

"I don't believe in religion."

"Well, then come up with something yourself, that is what I believe. Now you know what you have married into."

"Tir, I don't want to be Empress and die for it or die because you forced me to marry you."

"The gods chose you for me for a reason, only time will tell what our real destiny is. You did not seem to protest much in the last hours."

She raised her hand to slap him, he grabbed it strongly, "Don't you ever raise a hand to me like a barbarian, human." He saw the look of shock on her face and wanted to take back his racist comment but couldn't, he had already said it. He let go of her hand and she slapped him hard.

"Don't you ever call me a barbarian. You are the one who forced me to marry you. Sex is one thing, but marriage is an archaic and cruel practice which is why most of the galaxy as you know, illustrious Alliance Admiral, gave it up."

He looked at her and said evenly, "Kara, would you rather

I married you off to one of my junior officers? I could have. I thought you deserved better than that," and he wanted to add, 'And I have loved you since the moment I set eyes on you,' but instead said, "And I would not have trusted you to have married anyone who was less than your equal, otherwise I have no doubt, we would have a mini-revolution of human women on our hands in less than a couple of years." She still looked angry. "Kara, listen to me. This is what we are going to do. We are going to have fantastic sex. We are not going to be murdered by anyone. You are going to get a ship and we are going to save both the Alliance and human civilizations. We need human women to balance our numbers, but we will not take too many. The sooner we have a child, the better we can maybe figure out what has happened with our own women. In return, the Alliance will protect Earth and you must admit you need protection. The Alliance will allow humans to develop as they would choose, except for a few differences, women and protection. As my wife, you are not a pet, but for the moment you are still my prisoner. The sooner you accept your position, the sooner I can trust you and then you can start freely enjoying your new status in the galaxy as an Alliance citizen."

"I guess when you put it like that, it does not sound too terrible given my other option was probably death."

"Or marriage to someone you might hate. I know you don't hate me. We don't know each other well, but there is something between us. You do not have to believe in religion or destiny to feel that."

She nodded. "I just want to sleep now."

They got back into bed and he turned out the lights. He held her and after a long silence she said, "I think the gods sent me to you to keep you from being Emperor. I always want to be on a ship, out free in the galaxy."

"Me too," he agreed.

In the morning he woke up before her and got out of bed to check his ships' statuses. Nothing out of the ordinary had happened during the night. He made sure his junior lieutenant had her shoes made by the time he brought breakfast for them. When breakfast was laid out, he went into the bedroom to wake Kara. She was sleeping so soundly he did not want to wake her, but he knew that she would be upset if she missed another meal, so he said her name gently. She didn't stir. He touched her arm and she shooed him away. Then he picked her up and stood her up on her feet and instantly, she tried to get back into bed. He picked her up again and smacked her rear.

"Oww..." she murmured rubbing where he had smacked her. He saw she had some bruises from last night and he wanted to kiss those away but reminded himself that he would have to do that later as they had things to do this morning.

"I didn't want to wake you, but I knew you wouldn't want to miss breakfast." He left her standing naked next to the bed with her eyes closed. He went to his wardrobe and got out a clean dress for her and some warm, black stockings and handed it all to her.

She slowly began putting on her clothes. First the thigh-high stockings which felt nice and warm and then the navy dress. She struggled with the clasps and after some minutes had only managed three out of ten clasps before he came to her rescue. "It's better than yesterday," she commented, and he ignored her, "Thanks," she said when he had finished helping her.

He handed her the necklace he had given her to signify their marriage, "You should wear this."

"Everyday?"

"Alliance women would wear it often at intervals with the jewelry they already had."

"Okay, so I will skip today as my interval," she saw some disappointment cross his face and she couldn't believe it would mean so much to him. "It is heavy, and I am not used to wearing any kind of jewelry. Get me something much smaller and I will wear it daily, if that makes you happy."

"Your jewelry reflects my status. If I got you something small people might not think I am much more than a slave."

"How many Alliance men are married to human women?"

"One."

"One other than you?"

He shook his head and motioned his finger between them, "Only us."

"Good. Everyone will know I am your wife dressed in these clothes as I guarantee there is a good reason no other women in the galaxy ever willingly wear Alliance dresses and I need not wear any jewelry. But I do need shoes."

"You think Alliance dresses are unattractive?"

She looked at him in disbelief.

Just then the door chimed and the young man who was becoming a familiar fixture came in with shoes. He laid her new shoes in front of her. They were flat, black boots. They looked warm and comfortable. She put them on immediately and felt much better, almost good enough to wear his jewelry as she wanted to make him as happy as possible.

When the young man left, Kara asked, "What is his name?"

"Junior Lieutenant Mux, you can refer to him as Mux. Now let's eat."

Kara sat down to another bland breakfast of some form of bread and bland vegetables, like potatoes but with less texture if that was even possible. She was still very hungry though, so she ate everything and then asked, "Do you have coffee or tea? A warm drink?"

"No, we only have water or wine. On our capital planet we have begun importing human drinks and food. When you move there…"

She interrupted him, "I am not leaving you."

"I can only keep you here as long as the war continues. After that you will have to leave."

"No."

"We will discuss it when the time comes." He had not considered that she would want to remain with him. It was forbidden of course, but if he was being honest with himself, he never wanted her to leave either. "Now you must go to your ship and get your things, then inform your crew of their futures. I would prefer it if you wore the necklace, I gave you yesterday not for your crew but for mine. We are married."

She said nothing but nodded. They both rose, and he retrieved the necklace and put it on her. "Let's go," he said, and they walked out the door together trailed by four, large, heavily-armed Alliance guards.

"You are not taking any chances," she commented.

"You managed to take out more than one Alliance ship with your inferior vessel. One ship could have been luck, but any more than that was skill. I would never make the mistake of underestimating you, Kara."

They arrived at the docking bay and there was her *Dakota*. The Admiral and guards followed her onboard the old ship. She was not ashamed, it was a great ship and had served her well. She was sad to see it go without her. She went to her small quarters that was just a room with a bunk and a desk. Only the Admiral followed her in. She got down a bag and started putting clothes and things in it. She had an extra uniform and asked, "Do you mind if I wear this to speak to my crew, it might be the last time they see me for quite some time."

He stopped investigating things on her small desk and considered this. "Fine, but this is a favor I am doing for you, do not forget it. I will want something in return later."

She nodded and took off the dress and necklace and laid them politely on the bed as she took out a pair of underwear and a matching bra, she never thought she would be so happy to see and put them on. She specifically chose the one sexy pair she had onboard, thinking he may like them.

"What are those things," he asked looking at her bra and underwear with slight disgust.

"Undergarments. Human women like them. They make us feel comfortable."

"They look unattractive. If you wear them under your Alliance dresses, I will cut them off so they will be ruined." She turned around and gave him a skeptical look, "I am just warning you."

"I would love to see you use your sword actually, so I might just do that later." She smiled to herself thinking Alliance men probably found the ugly dress I had on before attractive if they think black lace bras and underwear are unattractive. She put on her red uniform then and zipped it up. She felt better. Then she put the dress and necklace in her bag with her other things. She also was sure to grab some old-fashioned pictures of her parents from her desk, a book, her computer, and all her other personal things. Then she turned to him, "We are going to take some coffee and tea too, come on," and she led him to the mess where she pillaged not only coffee and tea but some spices as well.

"Is that everything?" Tir asked. She nodded. Then he motioned for one of his guards to take her things, "Take Captain Kara's things to my quarters."

"That's not my name," she admonished.

"Your family name is now the same as mine and we do not use family names in general conversation, so yes that is your name. Come."

She said nothing because they entered the brig then. She addressed her male crew first. She was surprised to see even more guards enter the room behind them.

Her crew all saluted her, no doubt they had heard what had happened, that she had been forced into marriage with the Admiral to save their lives.

"All male members of the crew *Dakota* will return to Earth and not participate in this war any further as terms of the agreement I have made with the Alliance Admiral Tir." Then their forcefield went down and they were hastily escorted away by the extra guards before she could even say proper goodbyes. She made eye contact with all of her men as they walked by her in a single file line. Their faces all said one thing to her, 'This is not over, Captain.'

Kara then turned to her female crew that was in the holding cell next to where the men had been kept. She looked at them, some of them so young with their whole lives in front of them, now she was just giving them to the Alliance for the barbaric practice of marriage. But she reminded herself quickly, *We could all be dead so this is better than death, I think.*

"All female crew of the *Dakota* will be sent to the Alliance capital planet to be married to Alliance men. They have a demographics problem. We must sacrifice ourselves to preserve humanity. I have been assured that if we cooperate, less human women will be taken." She had been assured of no such thing, but she couldn't tell these young women that they were just being taken as wives. "Alliance men will treat you with respect and there are laws to protect you. Ask for new translators so you can read and stay in contact with each other. Be strong and be proud to be human. They need us more than we need them right now, don't forget that. I will find you all." Then another group of guards led them quickly away at the Admiral's nod. Most had tears in their eyes as they passed her and she was sure to look all of the women in the eye as they passed her with a confident face and attitude, even though that was the last thing she was feeling. Kara felt guilty and silently vowed that she would escape and free them from this Alliance slavery, even if it took years or the rest of her life. Human women were owned by no one.

PRISONER

C aptain Kara Rainer had just sent her crew off in separate directions. The men back to Earth in her ship, *No, their ship now*, she thought remorsefully, *the Dakota*. Their only condition was that they had to make an oath to the Alliance, in the person of Admiral Tir, not to participate in this war with the Jahay anymore. This was an easy agreement to make. Humans were the most underdeveloped civilization in the known galaxy. They had spent more time on their exports of art, music and exotic cuisine than military strength. They had been bullied into the war between the Alliance and the Jahay.

However, her female crew was not so lucky. They were being sent to the Alliance's capital planet to be wives, an archaic and barbaric societal ritual that only the Alliance and a few other civilizations in the galaxy still practiced. Apparently, the Alliance had a secret demographics issue and they needed women. Unfortunately for Kara and her female crew, the only other species that were compatible with Alliance citizens were humans. Kara herself had already been forced to marry Admiral Tir of the starship *Refa* which they were now on, but unlike the rest of her female crew, she was staying with him onboard. He was going to use her to help win the war as she was privy to relevant information about Jahay strategies and weaponry. The Admiral tried to reassure her that her female crew would be taken care of and live well in the Alliance. He talked about human women now being Alliance citizens and equality between the sexes, but Kara knew how racist the Alliance was against aliens and she could already see that the Alliance may have granted human women full-citizenship in theory only. She guessed that human women would still be outlanders in their society. And if any half-Alliance, half-human children were produced she shuddered to think where their place would be in Alliance society. She watched the last woman walk into the transport that would take them to the supply ship and sighed, "It is better than being dead, I suppose," she said more to herself than the Admiral who was standing next to her.

"They will have good lives and if you all assimilate soon you will be together again working on a starship," he said frankly. "Better lives than you could have had on Earth I think."

"Why do you keep saying that?" she was trying to keep her voice down and not get emotional. "Earth is our home. Not everything in life is about being the best at everything. We are human. I am human. My heart will always long for Earth." She looked up at him, he was a bit shocked by her little speech. "You better get used to hearing that as it will not change as long as I am alive. And you will see Earth and you will love it too." She did not know why she added that last part about him loving Earth too, she was going to try to escape, *Aren't I?* she questioned herself.

He smiled then, "Okay Kara. Alliance citizenship is a gift. You must begin to come to some compromise in your heart," he lightly touched her chest where her heart was, then turned and began walking away.

She looked at him with animosity on her face. When she didn't follow him immediately, the guards pushed her forward a little then she started walking behind him. Kara was cross with him for everything now. She wished she was heading back to Earth with her entire crew, not here married to this alien, not sending her female crew off to be alien brides. Of course, she was especially upset with herself for liking him so much, for enjoying his touch so much in the middle of this whole mess. She hated herself in that moment because she felt she had let her whole crew down and she enjoyed being with him when they were alone. She wondered then if they had drugged her to feel this way.

Tir was amused by her little speech about being human. He liked her pride and loyalty to her own, despite them being so lowly in the galaxy. He knew that when he had earned her respect and trustworthiness it would be real. He knew that she would try to pretend but her personality was such that she would never be able to pretend for long and he was glad for that. He made his way now to the conference room. He was going to have a strategy meeting with all his captains, he wanted Kara to be there to put her on the spot about Jahay locations and ships. He had purposely not told her about this so that she would have no time to prepare adequate lies. He only wished he could have kept more than her doctor behind as a hostage to hold over her head, but he figured Doctor John would do and that in the long run, it would be better for the Alliance and Kara that he showed some compassion towards the humans for a better long-term relationship.

Kara realized after a couple minutes of walking that they were not returning to his quarters and then began to wonder where they were going. Her mind was racing with possibilities, all of them terrible. It crossed her mind that he was going to torture her for information about the war and the Jahay. She did not have much information, but she did have some and now that her crew was gone, he had very little leverage over her. She wondered then if he thought she would just tell him what he wanted, she reckoned he would be arrogant enough to think so. One thing was clear for her though, she had no loyalty to the Jahay. True they had never taken Earth as a slave planet, but they had forced humanity into their war and it was because of them, she and her crew were now in this strange situation with the Alliance. And another truth was that the Admiral had saved her entire crew, granted he had ulterior motives for the women, but he had still saved them and allowed the men to return to Earth unharmed. So, she did not know where she stood about telling him information about the Jahay and the war. She decided she would wait and see how he asked the question.

When they arrived at the large conference room with a table and twenty some chairs all occupied with Alliance officers, she then knew what was going on. There were two chairs empty, one at the head of the table and the other next to it on the side. Tir pointed to a chair next to his for Kara to sit down and she sat without speaking. She was just happy she was wearing her uniform to show that she was not just some human woman married to Admiral Tir. She hated the idea of being married. She could not help but look back defiantly at all the curious Alliance men who were intriguingly looking at her. Although they all had the same color grey skin and long black hair, just like humans, their facial features varied. She then looked up at Tir and thought, *Good, I don't just find you attractive because you are exotic to me as an Alliance, you actually are good-looking among your people too. Unless symmetry and strength are not considered good-looking?* she almost smiled thinking about her little joke to herself.

Tir did not look at Kara but instead addressed his captains, "As you all know the last battle with the Jahay was a success." He brought up a virtual map above the conference room table of this section of the galaxy with Alliance and Jahay ships marked. He began discussing the battle, fast-forwarding through to different events, stopping at different times to talk about how things had happened to either criticize or praise some of his captains. Kara was surprised that he even mentioned her ship at one point in criticism against one of his captains for letting her get so close as to do a bit of damage. She was even more surprised that he turned to her then and said, "That was well done, Captain. You have a brave crew considering had my Captain been faster to react you would not be sitting here with us now." After many minutes he then talked about where they thought the Jahay might have regrouped to and what their strategy might be for the next battle and the rest of the war. Then he looked at Kara and said, "Captain Kara, please show us where they have regrouped on the map."

She looked up at him without expression, "I am sorry they did not tell lowly humans where they might be. We were only given coordinates after, if we survived a battle or reconnaissance mission."

"Captain, your doctor is still in our brig. Does that refresh your memory?"

She sighed. She looked at the small virtual console in front of her on the table and tried to figure out how to bring up the coordinates, but without her handheld translator she could not make out the Alliance written language. So, she stood up and pointed to the places on the large virtual map that was displayed across the long table.

Tir was pleased that she did it. He also enjoyed watching her walk around the table in her tight red uniform. He still had his fantasy about her wearing that. He also could not help but notice that his men appreciated her attractive curves and appearance as well as she walked around the table and pointed out different coordinates.

Kara returned to her seat and more plans were made. She was less cross with Tir the longer the meeting went on. She watched and listened to him discuss the progress of the war with his captains. His men seemed to respect him in a way that she found a bit cold, but she reasoned that it could just be their culture, Alliance people were not known for their warm personalities. Sitting in the meeting not really being expected to participate again she could just watch him. He was tall, even for an Alliance man and unlike many of the other men, who wore their hair in a braid or multiple braids, he always wore his loose and she wondered if this was a status hairstyle. Then she remembered how thick it was and longed to touch it again as it also smelled of him, like petrichor with a bit of mint. Inevitably, her mind ran to sex and then to his expectations of her as a wife. Kara wondered what kind of culture the Alliance really was. She knew so little about it. There were the rumors around the galaxy of course, that they were all quite brutal, archaic with their ideas about honor and women. She knew women rarely left the Alliance planets and were forbidden from serving in their military. She wondered if he really would give her an Alliance ship once she gained his trust. She had no reason to doubt him. He had not lied to her yet and if the Alliance really needed human women and not as sex slaves, it was better to entice humans with what they needed, which was more technology. It occurred to her then that maybe that was the Alliance's plan all along, to begin with the women serving in the starships and have a kind of trickle-down effect to women on Earth who might even come freely to be wives in the Alliance. She had some friends back home that read a lot of old romance novels and that would probably love to be married again, even to a man with grey skin that lived on a colder and darker planet.

Tir asked Kara a question then and she almost missed it as she was daydreaming about her friends at home. "Captain Kara, how many Class One Warships does the Jahay have in sector two?"

She looked at the virtual map and found sector two. It was difficult for her to remember. She closed her eyes trying to remember the maps she had seen. "I believe only one, Admiral."

"You are sure?"

"As sure as I can be for only seeing the information once three days ago."

"Good enough."

He was finishing his well-organized meeting now. Kara was surprised that all his captains rose and bowed to him after he formally ended the meeting with a religious prayer. She stood, but was not going to bow to him, although she could not deny that she was completely aroused that he did command so much respect from his men and was not a complete idiot. Despite whatever rank he had been born into in his society, he definitely had earned this position of Admiral, which she was glad of. She could never have been with someone that was an idiot. But then she reminded herself she probably could have escaped already if she had been forced to marry an idiot and then questioned her own emotions, *Come on Rainer, you can't start thinking about the future with him or becoming emotionally attached. You have got to keep him happy, gain his trust and then escape.*

Tir ended the meeting and then waited for everyone to leave. He sent his guards outside the door and then locked it. He walked directly over to Kara then and just began fervently kissing her.

She was so surprised. Kara had not expected him to just come to her with so much desire, here in the conference room, only 30 seconds after he had just finished a meeting. But after a couple minutes of kissing each other, she didn't care that they were in the conference room and his guards were right outside. His hands were on her hips pushing her body against his, she could feel that he was aroused already, and his tongue was exploring every inch of her mouth. She knew this would be different than the sex they had had in his quarters, that this was definitely fantasy sex. But she did not mind, she had thought he was so sexy while he talked about the battle the other day and strategies.

Her suspicions were confirmed when he said, "Ever since I saw you in here yesterday, I wanted to do this," he admitted. "And watching you walk around the map with your fitted uniform and all my captain's eyes on you was so intoxicating."

"You do realize Tir, that this is your favor for letting me wear my uniform."

"I know," he said between kisses. "Why do you think I agreed so easily when you asked to take off the dress and put on your uniform?"

"You had this planned?"

"Only since you asked to put on your uniform about an hour ago," he easily lifted her up onto the black conference room table and began unzipping her uniform. "And of course, I understood you did not want to be wearing a dress when you saw your crew off. Kara, I am not a complete brute. Although I have never had a prisoner before, I am trying to make this as civilized as possible."

Kara looked into his green eyes and said, "I don't think you can use the words 'civilized', 'prisoner' and 'wife' in the same sentence. But I will admit one thing, I love it when your hands are on me." She tried to wiggle off the table to better take off her uniform. "Wait, it's better if I stand up," she explained. He frowned but she jumped down and commanded him, "Sit."

He sat down in a chair and she stood in front of him about half a meter away, she was going to give him a little show she had decided as she was jumping down. One of her hands on her uniform zipper, innocently playing with it and looked at him and said, "I heard the Alliance never took prisoners. What are you going to do with me then? I don't want to die."

He picked up on the game immediately and liked her even more for this. "What do you have to offer human?"

"Well," she said slowly and began unzipping her uniform. When she reached her belly button, she smiled up at him seductively and said, "I've never been with an alien before. Should I be scared? You know there are all these rumors about Alliance men in the galaxy and I am just a little human woman, we don't mate outside our species." She was running her index finger up and down the sliver of exposed skin from where she had unzipped her uniform.

Tir was surprised she said that and wanted to say something clever and sexy back, but his mind was blank. "Let's take it slowly then so you don't get scared. Unzip the rest of your uniform."

She looked at him and then slowly ran her hands seductively over her body before she began slowly unzipping her uniform further. When she had it all the way unzipped, she turned around and looked over her shoulder at him while she slowly worked it off her shoulders and then said, "I've never done this before. I feel so naughty."

If he had not been so aroused, he would have laughed at that. He had the feeling that this was a show she had done many times before, *And why not? She was so sexy in that uniform.* "I give you permission to be as naughty as you want, Captain. Maybe it will help your situation here as my prisoner."

She put her finger in her mouth then and looked at him, then took it out and said, "As naughty as I want, Admiral? You have no idea how wicked my mind can be."

"Yes, whatever you want to do."

Kara still had her back to Tir, she slowly pulled the rest of her uniform down and stepped out of it. She was crouched down seductively and then ran her hands slowly up the back of her legs over her bottom, skimming her hips, through her short, brown hair until her arms were high above her head. After a couple seconds, she lowered her hands to rest on the back of her neck and looked back at him again. Then she ran her hands back down to her black lace underwear and began rubbing her rear. There were some bruises there. "As you can see, I have already been so naughty and adequately punished for it." Then she began pulling her underwear up to cause some friction against her clitoris and anus. Then she ran two fingers over her pulled underwear and said, "But I can't help it. I am just so naughty."

"You will have to show me more if that is what you really want."

She gave him a feigned look of confusion, "I will do my best." Then she turned and put her hand down the front of her underwear and stroked herself while she bit her lip and looked at him with innocent eyes, "I am so wet already thinking about having an alien penis inside of me."

Tir was impressed with her little show and he did not want it to stop. "Keep touching yourself like that and I promise I will pump into your vagina so hard you will never want to have sex with a human again. You will only desire me."

"Are you sure? I mean how do you know? Have you ever been with a human?" she said coming closer, "You know, we have all these curves," she ran her hands down over her hips on to her bottom. "And we have breasts," she touched her breasts over her bra until she could see that they were hard with arousal. "And we have hair, do you want to see?"

"I want to see your nether hair," he replied.

She gave him a coy look, "What if you don't like it? I will be so desperate sex and embarrassed."

"I will like it. I promise."

"You promise to still have sex with me? I need you inside of me. I have been so naughty. Throughout the whole meeting, I was looking at you, thinking about you, hoping that maybe you would find me attractive enough to have sex with. And I was fantasizing about you taking me right here on the table during your meeting."

He had noticed that towards the end of the meeting she was no longer looking at him with scorn but with desire. "I promise, I will still have sex with you. Show me the hair on your body. I want to see it and run my fingers through it."

She slowly bent down in front of him again, she was so close to where he was sitting, her rear almost touched his knees. She slowly pulled her underwear down giving him a nice view of her bottom. Then she stood up slowly and turned around her hands over her vulva. Her head was down in feigned embarrassment.

He could not take much more of this, she was driving him crazy. He could smell her desire. "Show me. I promise I will still want to have sex with you. Show me your hair."

She slowly moved her hands away and once she did that, he pulled her to him and began kissing her passionately. He ripped off the bra and was sucking her nipples as if he had never seen them before. In no time he had her up on the conference table and was kissing her all while his finger was moving rhythmically over her clitoris in a way that he was finding worked for her here and now. He loved watching her and knew that she was close to coming. He whispered in her ear, "You are so wicked. I love running my fingers through this human hair. Be my naughty wife."

"Barbarian," she whispered breathlessly and then she came.

"I adore your face when I make you come. You are the goddess herself," he whispered in her ear before he tore down his trousers. He entered her and was quickly and forcefully pumping into her. Her legs were on either side of him and he was holding her back, enjoying the sight of her as he thrust into her again and again. After some minutes, he flipped her over and held her hands behind her back, "You're so wicked Kara, I bet this is going to make you come again." He knew that from this angle and her breasts pressed against the cold table, there was a chance he could make her come again. Especially if he held her hands behind her back strongly.

She could not believe that he was pounding into her on the conference room table like this right after a meeting. She knew it was his arrogance, but then she thought, He *is right, he is going to make me come again, oh ecstasy.* She wondered if she would ever be able to leave if every day, they were going to have sex like this. She hated herself for loving this so much and for not being able to turn him down. But then she told her conscience, *Oh be quiet and enjoy this, you could be dead, we will think about morals later.*

He climaxed shortly after she did a second time and pulled out of her. Semen and her own wetness dripped from her empty vagina now. She sat up. He pulled up his trousers and then grabbed her uniform from the floor.

"No, I need to put on my underwear first," she instructed him, and he handed her the black lace underwear. She put on her underwear to somewhat stop the flow of semen running down her legs, and then looked around for her bra which he had thrown in the heat of the moment. She jumped down and went across the room.

"Where are you going?"

She picked up her bra off the floor and held it up to him as an answer and then put it on. He brought her uniform over to her.

They had made a mess of sweat and sex on the table, "Should we clean that up?"

"No."

"Tir, it's not like we spilt some water."

"I don't understand you Kara. You are my wife. Everyone onboard knows we are just married as well. For a culture that does not get married anymore, you can be very prude. I will send the slaves in to clean the table."

"You keep slaves onboard?"

He looked at her and realized there was still so much she didn't know about Alliance culture. "Yes. I will tell you about it over the midday meal. Right now, I need to return you to our quarters because I have some actual work to do." He could not help himself but ran his fingers through her hair as he looked into her big brown eyes. "Thank you for helping with the Jahay strategies."

"How do you know I was not lying?"

"Because I already knew where they were located from intelligence, I received this morning. You just confirmed it."

Kara looked up at him trying to decide if he was lying but, in the end, could not determine whether he was lying. She did not know him well enough yet and he was too clever to be a terrible liar she mused. They walked back to his quarters in silence, his men would greet him as they passed and look at her curiously.

Tir walked her back to his quarters and escorted her in, "All your possessions from your ship are here. I will do my best to keep you onboard the *Refa* with me as long as possible. Take your things and put them where you will. This is our space now." He paused then considering and then finally said after a couple of minutes, "And I know you are going to go through my things because that is what I would do. There are swords in the bottom of my wardrobe. Do not bother trying to use one to try and escape if you never have used a sword before. It will just be annoying, and I will not even punish you for it. There is nothing else of interest. I will be back soon."

Kara just watched him walk away leaving her in all astonishment, *Swords in his closet? What was he a knight?* Of course, the first thing she did was go check out the swords in the bottom of his wardrobe and sure enough in the black and yellow boxes there were short swords like the one he wore. She went to find her handheld translator and held it over a lot of the engravings on the swords to see what they said. She got bored after a while, they were all just for his different ranks through the military. There was nothing surprising about them at all. She put them all back then and went to her bag and things and got out the small painting her father had painted for her of the beach near their house at sunset. She put it next to what she would assume would be her side of the bed as she slept on that side last night.

Then she sat on the bed looking at the small painting thinking, *Will I ever be there again to see a sunset on that beach?* She became very sad and was happy she was alone because she needed a good cry for all that had happened in the last weeks and especially in the last 24 hours and the shower was way too cold to have a good proper cry in. She cried for being married, losing her ship and half of her crew and for not dying when maybe she should have instead of accepting this marriage deal. And then she cried for humanity for wasting so much time on frivolous things instead of military, technology and defense. After she had cried for all those things, she wiped her eyes and felt much better.

She went into the bathroom to splash some water on her face and the mirror began talking to her again. "Good afternoon Kara. Would you like the water warmer? It is currently set for Tir."

"Leave me alone mirror. I don't like smart mirrors."

"Do you need some help shaping your eyebrows?" the mirror asked.

"What is wrong with my eyebrows?" Kara asked touching one of them looking in the mirror. She had never done anything to her eyebrows, she had always considered them one of her natural beauties.

"I can recommend different shapes..." the mirror suggested, and Kara interrupted.

"Absolutely not. Can you tell me when my next period is going to begin and what Alliance women do for that?" Human women still used a menstrual cup because humanity was all about being close to nature, but she suspected with all this technology, Alliance women would have something much better.

"Processing," the mirror said and then after about a minute

continued, "Kara, I have insufficient data to confirm your next period as you have only been aboard a short amount of time. Please seek advice from sickbay on deck five section two."

"What can you actually tell me then, mirror?"

"I can tell you many things. Ask me a question."

"How many women has Tir brought to his quarters in the last year?"

"Admiral Tir has brought three slave women to his quarters in the last year."

"What?"

"Admiral Tir has brought three slave women to his quarters in the last year."

"I heard you. Turn off mirror," she said as she went to go sit on the toilet and take all of this information in. *Slave women*, she thought to herself and felt a bit sick.

When she finished in the bathroom she went into the sitting room, armed with her handheld translator and turned on his computer. She tried to bring up any basic files on the *Refa's* crew compliment but was locked out of almost everything, but internal communication and she knew that was on purpose. Then she got out her own computer and began looking for the little cultural information humans had about the Alliance. She scanned through all the statistics until she found the part about slaves, but it just said that the Alliance had a class of slaves. She slammed the button to close her virtual computer and thought, *Useless.*

Kara sat in silence in the sitting room then and thought about her emotions. Why was she so upset? Was it because he was with other women before her or because they were slaves or was it both? She thought about it for many minutes and concluded that it was both. She had to admit to herself that she was infatuated with him and she was jealous, even though these feelings were ridiculous because she had just met him. Then she was upset that his culture had slaves and that he had taken advantage of his position to be intimate with them, she imagined rape. But it was difficult for her to imagine him raping someone given that he was a very considerate lover, he did not seem like the type, but then she reminded herself you never really know about people until they have committed the crime.

Mux chimed the door and then came in without Kara saying anything. He greeted her and explained he had brought the midday meal and would lay it out in the dining room. After he had finished, he told Kara that Admiral Tir was on his way soon, to join her.

"I just have one question Mux."

He stopped and looked at Kara.

"How many slaves are onboard and how many of the slaves are women?"

"I don't know exactly. At least 100 slaves and probably 35 of them are women."

"And why are the women onboard?"

"They are artists," he said as if that explained everything.

"I didn't think the Alliance produced any kind of art," she said suspiciously.

"No, artists in that they recite some of the ancient myths, dance and provide basic entertainment."

"Entertainment? For money?"

He nodded, "Of course, Captain. Is there anything else?"

"No, thank you."

It was not long before Tir returned and he was pleased that she had waited for him to begin eating. "Shall we eat now?"

"Wait. I want to ask you about something."

He could tell she was annoyed about something, but he was perplexed about what could possibly be bothering her as she had just been sitting in his quarters for the last 40 minutes putting her things in order.

"I was talking to the mirror," she began and realized she sounded like a crazy person but tried to hurry past that fact and be serious, "And it said that you had three slave women in here this past year. Explain to me why you would need to rape a slave woman?"

It took all his self-control not to laugh at her from getting jealous from what the bathroom mirror had reported to her. "Kara, I would never rape a woman. I am offended that you would even think that. Second, these slave women are here of their own free will and they do not do anything that they do not want to do, ask any man on this ship. Not only that, they are making a lot of universal credits off us all. I can ask one to come and join us now if you do not believe me? They recite ancient myths, history and battle stories. They keep us all sane when we are so far from home and our families."

"Why are they called 'slaves' then if they are here of their own free will?"

"It is an old class marker and maybe thousands of years ago they were slaves in the true sense of the word, but no longer. They own land, have their own money and control their own destinies as far as the gods allow for any of us."

"But what about the Alliance's slave planets?"

"That is a completely different thing. But still no one is raping anyone there that I know of. I have never raped anyone, and I do not know of anyone who has committed rape or been raped. We do marry, and I understand that you find this barbaric, but we do not rape. Understand? Can we eat?"

She stood up, "I am still uncomfortable, three women Tir?"

He put his hand on her shoulder, "We have been married for one day and you are jealous about three women I had to pay to come here over the last year? Shouldn't you be feeling sorry for me?"

She frowned, "I am not jealous about the women as much as I am that you paid them." But if she was being honest, she was jealous about thinking of him with someone else.

He looked at her and didn't know what to say for a minute, this was a normal part of his culture and no one had ever questioned him about it. "I did not have an emotional connection with any of the women, it was just sex." He almost smiled then remembering the threesome he had with Sera and the doctor.

Kara looked at him and didn't know what to say. Prostitution was legal on Earth, of course it was, but she herself had never bought sex, but then again, she had never been in the position to have to either. "Why did you do it?"

"Pay for sex?"

"Yes."

"Because I was single, bored and had been off-planet for many weeks. These slave artists choose their positions. They are famous throughout the Alliance, they cost a small fortune and pray on the men that are off-planet for long periods of time."

"You make it sound like you are the victim here."

"No one is a victim," he looked at her and thought he was explaining this all wrong. "This is a matter of consumerism. I don't understand why you are upset."

"Do you plan to still sleep with those slave artists now that you are married?"

"Only if you want to."

"Like a threesome?"

He nodded.

"I can't suck your penis until I'm pregnant, but threesomes are okay? What kind of gods are the Alliance worshiping?"

"Threesomes only with other women until you are pregnant," he clarified as if that would make more sense to her.

"You must be joking?" Kara let out a laugh then. Then her mind was racing, "So what about orgies?"

"All the same rules apply," he said not understanding how strange this sexual practice was for her.

She looked at him and laughed again.

"I don't understand why you are laughing. Should I call a slave artist here now? I would not mind seeing one again," he suggested provocatively.

"No," she said adamantly through her laughter. "I cannot believe that you get married but then still sleep with these slave artists. What sense does that make?"

"A lot of sense. How do you track your ancestry on Earth if not through marriage? Humans do not have a large population. Aren't you worried about incest?"

"We do not have a problem with incest. We are not beasts. We always run genetic tests at special centers before we decide to have children together."

He was suspicious now, "How do you begin to have children? Certainly, it must just happen with a lot of the population?"

"We are all on birth control until we decide not to be."

"Women take birth control? Are you on birth control now and you didn't say anything?"

"It is technically still in my system yes, unless your doctor did something to make it inactive? I was going to mention it when you mentioned getting pregnant but then you took my breath away the first time, we were having sex. Afterwards, I forgot I had not told you. We have only been married for a day." She could see on his face he was annoyed with her.

He rose, took her arm gently and escorted her down to sick-bay. Kara was surprised to see her own doctor John there working with Doctor Siu.

Siu looked up when they walked in and excused himself from John and escorted Tir and Kara into a private room. "Is something the matter?"

"Apparently human women are on birth control."

Kara was surprised the doctor looked so horrified by this information. He then politely asked Kara to lay down on the medical bed and began running a handheld device over her, looking at the results on the little screen.

Kara was watching Siu and remembered how he watched her have sex with Tir at their marriage ceremony, if you could call it a marriage ceremony. Then, she could not help but wonder, *Did you go find one of these slave artists and have sex with her imagining it was me, Doctor?* She had to admit to herself she was aroused again thinking about him watching her and then she wondered, *Do his scans tell him I am aroused too?*

Siu was good at blocking thoughts out that did not concern him. He had to be. Most doctors in the Unification were bred to be empaths and telepathic and Siu was no exception. But he decided he could listen to Kara's thoughts because they did concern him, and he had to use all his self-control not to smile and say, 'No, my machines don't tell me you are aroused, but your eyes and thoughts do, and I would happily watch you have sex again.'

Siu finished running scans and professionally said, "The human birth control is at such a low dosage, it would not inhibit Alliance men from impregnating human women, but I will remove it from her system and let our doctors know of the situation on the capital planet." He looked at Kara then and said sympathetically, "I'm sorry that you were ever put on birth control. I cannot imagine what a backwards place Earth is."

Kara was very confused now. She sat up, "What are you talking about?"

"Women's bodies are sacred, you are the bringers of life. To interfere with women's health is to interfere with the gods," explained the doctor. "In addition, from a biological point of view, it is much less invasive to have men use metabolized birth control."

"No Alliance women take birth control?"

"Only slave artists as they have a special agreement with the gods."

Of course, they do, thought Kara. She could not believe she was going to have this conversation with a doctor but then decided that he had watched her have sex with a man she was forced to marry so there was nothing professional about their relationship. "Do people only have sex with slave artists before marriage then?"

"No."

She looked from Tir to Siu and waited for more information and when she didn't get it after a minute she asked, "Are you going to explain this then?" Then she looked at Tir, "I am assuming you are not on birth control?"

He looked at her annoyed, "No, let's go. I will explain all of this later." He wanted to go and eat.

"Wait," she said to Tir and then looking at Siu asked, "What do Alliance women do about their periods? As you might have guessed, we are very old-fashioned on Earth."

Siu looked at her and could see in her mind the shape of a small cup filled with blood. "We have a little device Alliance women call, 'the tab'. I know that we have some here in sickbay, but I will have to look for them. When I find one, I will call for you and show you how to use it. I think it will be much more convenient than your cup."

"How did you know?" she trailed off and Siu smiled at her.

"Alliance doctors can read your thoughts."

Kara blushed then.

Tir and Siu smiled at each other and Tir did not have to wonder too much what she had been thinking about that made her blush.

"Wife, do you have any more questions for the doctor?" Tir asked with a bit of humor to his voice.

She smiled at them both from a little embarrassment, "No, I think I have asked enough for today. Thank you and do not forget to look for that tab, Doctor."

When they walked out of the private room in sickbay, Kara looked for Doctor John as she wanted to speak to him, but he was nowhere to be seen. Then she asked Siu who was behind them, "Where has Doctor John gone?"

"He has gone to eat the midday meal. Should I call him back?"

"No, I will speak to him later," she was so hungry herself she wanted to eat too. Kara and Tir left sickbay and began walking back to his quarters, "I am starving."

"I hate to tell you this, but we have missed the meal."

"No, what are you talking about? The food will still be there, right?"

"No, Mux would have taken it away. We must wait until evening now."

"You have got to be kidding."

"Kara, next time you want to talk about something wait until after we have eaten."

"So, we have missed the meal, what about Siu did he also

miss the meal?"

"Yes. If I come in there, he has to attend to me whether it is mealtime or not."

"Why didn't you say something? I would have much rather eaten lunch than question you about women from your past."

"Good. You will remember this then. I thought I made it clear yesterday, but maybe I should not have allowed you to eat when it was not a time for eating sanctioned by the gods."

When they entered his quarters, she went immediately to check the dining room and sure enough there was not a bit of food to be found there. She did pour herself a cup of wine, "I am so hungry. How long until the next meal?"

"Six hours."

She took her cup into the sitting room and he gave her a disapproving look, "What now?"

"No food or drink outside the dining room," he said and thought, *Gods, humans are barbaric.*

She went back into the dining room sat down with her cup and looked at him through the doorway. He sat on the sofa and began reading something on his communicator as if everything was fine. And she wondered then how often he had missed a meal and gone without food and that is why he was so fit. No doubt there would be countless times that he was busy with work and would miss the meal. She felt sorry for him then and all these Alliance men, they must be so hungry all the time.

She drank her wine and then poured herself another cup and wondered again how difficult it would be to escape. How she would even begin to plan such a thing. His guards were always outside and even if she could get past them and get to a transport, she couldn't get far, his ships were too powerful. She resigned herself then that she would have to learn the language and gain his trust, unless another opportunity wildly presented itself out of the blue, but she doubted that happening. She finished her second cup of wine and reckoned it would probably take her having a baby for him to trust her. And if that was what she was going to have to do, that is exactly what she would do.

She had to get home and back to Earth. She would not allow her emotions to get in the way.

But she looked at him and questioned herself, *Are you strong enough to have a baby and just leave it with him? What kind of man is he? Would he kill it? Could I escape with a baby too?* She thought about all this while she watched him quietly reading something on the sofa.

After she finished her cup of wine, she joined him in the sitting room. He looked up at her as she sat down. "Better now?"

"I am not a child."

"Don't act like one then," he admonished her.

"Humans eat whenever they want. We have meal times of course, but they are more just guidelines."

He put down what he was reading and looked into her brown eyes, "And now you are an Alliance citizen and you will act in a civilized manner."

She held his gaze for a long time, she could not believe he had again suggested humans were uncivilized. She thought to herself, *You carry a sword, practice marriage rituals and still believe in religion and you are calling me uncivilized?* But she said nothing to him for some many minutes, then she asked, "Can you teach me some Alliance written words so that I can better work simple things? Or you could reconsider and just give me a proper translator? I am your wife after all."

"You are my wife, but you are also my prisoner. I will introduce you to the program we give to children learning to read." He opened a virtual program on the small table between them. He flipped through the menu, she could not help but smile when she noticed that the last thing, he had used this table for looked like some kind of strategy game.

"Do you like games?" she asked.

"Yes, do you know how to play Uki?" It was an Alliance strategy game, many people in the galaxy knew how to play it. He had no illusions that he would be able to win against her once she learned to play.

"No, I have only heard about it, but I would like to learn."

"I will teach you, but now it is better if you learn to read a little first. I have no intention of giving you an Alliance translator soon, especially after you failed to mention the birth control."

"We have been married for one day Tir."

"And how many times did I make it clear, we need to have a child? I know you are far from being a fool, so do not take me for one either."

"Show me how to work the children's reading program," she said wanting to change the subject.

The learning program spoke to her as if she was a very young child, but it was perfect in explaining their written language. It was unfortunate that Alliance was not entirely phonetical, but she was not completely put off by that. Many of Earth's ancient cultures had not used phonetical writing systems. Once she listened to the explanation in English and it went through all the hieroglyphics in the first chapter, she mentally turned off her embedded translator and listened to it all again in Alliance. When she heard Alliance spoken, she was disheartened, it was tonal and there were so many tones, at least more than five. It was then that she realized that learning Alliance was not going to be as easy as she thought. But she thought she might as well learn it as just as every civilization in the galaxy, there were locks on high-security weapons and information that were only accessible to native speakers, even humans had them, even though no one had ever tried to take anything except some art from humans. Tir said something to her then but she didn't understand him because her translator was off. "Sorry, what did you say? I was concentrating."

"It shouldn't take you long to learn the core hieroglyphics and our complementary phonetics, Alliance children learn to read at a basic level in 30 weeks."

"And your great civilization never thought about a completely phonetical alphabet? Our children learn to read in days."

He shrugged, "What is 30 weeks of study in a child's schooling? And just because human children can pronounce all the words after a few days does not mean they know them. It is just a different way." He had never had to defend his written language to an alien before and felt defensive.

"True," she smiled at him, "Now let me get back to the first hieroglyphs."

He didn't smile back but thought, *Gods, let me not be so taken in with how adorable my wife is every second of the day even when she is so uncivilized or questioning of Alliance culture.* He decided then that after she had finished chapter two, he was going to take her in the bedroom and then in the shower. Then they would have the evening meal and he would have a slave artist visit them afterwards.

Kara finished the second chapter and was about ready to begin the third when Tir interrupted her by showing her a hieroglyphic on his communicator.

She didn't recognize it, "Should I have learned that one?"

He smiled, "No they definitely do not teach it to young children."

"Sex?"

"Close. Try again."

"Orgy."

"No."

"Anal sex."

"No and we can't do that until…"

She interrupted him, "I don't want your ridges going in there, ever."

"Some women enjoy…"

"Not me. A finger occasionally maybe but that is all. No ridges ever do you hear me?"

He smiled at her, "I understand, it's not something I really prefer. But maybe in the future you might want it. Have you figured out the word on my communicator yet?"

"Just tell me what that word is, you are totally getting me out of the mood talking about anal sex."

"Masturbation."

She laughed a little, "Why are you showing me that?"

"I want to watch you masturbate."

She began to get excited by the idea, "So while I was trying to learn how to read Alliance that is what you were thinking about?"

He nodded. She was his wife and he wanted to know her inside and out. If he could not bring her to climax, as fast as he could himself after a year, he would feel that he was failing her as a lover. Part of his understanding would definitely come from him watching her pleasure herself.

Kara got up and went into the bedroom. She looked at him, "Do you want me to wear my uniform as you had that fantasy earlier?"

"No, just naked. I will turn up the heat to 19C in the bedroom." He was so pleased she would do this. Most Alliance women would have made him wait a year if not more as they would feel they were giving their secrets away that men should have to work for.

She took off her uniform and immediately the cold air grabbed onto every nerve in her skin and gave her goosebumps. She got on the bed and lay back on the smart blankets that were thankfully already heating up to make her back feel warmer. When she knew he was watching she closed her eyes and began touching herself lightly with a finger.

Not more than a couple minutes passed before he said, gently and softly, "No Kara, touch yourself like I am not here."

She opened her eyes and looked at him, green eyes met brown, "Okay, but then I want to flip onto my stomach."

He smiled and thought to himself, *Yes, I thought so*. Then he got up and lay down next to her. Although it was difficult to see her hands, he could still sense the movements.

He was far enough away that she could not kiss him, but if she reached her hand out, she could easily touch him. She lay flat on her stomach and began touching her clitoris with her right hand, gently, then as the minutes went by, she increased the speed and pressure. By the time about 15 minutes had passed, she was quickly caressing her clitoris with big, strong circles. He turned her a bit to the side then as he knew that she would only welcome his mouth on her breasts then and she came within minutes.

"Happy?" she asked while he was still casually sucking on her left nipple.

"Yes," he touched her cheek, "You're face gets so pink after you come. It's beautiful."

She moved her naked body closer to his clothed body and he wrapped his arms around her. She lay her head against his shoulder. He caressed her soft, brown hair as he liked to do, and they said nothing for a while. Then he began caressing other areas of her body and she wanted him again. She looked up and they kissed. He used his teeth to grab gently at her bottom lip and she began quickly undressing him but could not manage to get his jewelry off, but she didn't care, she needed him now.

Tir hovered over her, his necklaces falling down against her breasts and torso. He spread her bent legs wide as he slowly entered her vagina. She tried to grab him to make him change positions, so he would enter her with more force, but he shook his head.

"Touch yourself now. I want to watch you again."

"I can't," she said, thinking there was no way she could orgasm again.

"It doesn't matter if you don't come again, it makes me so aroused to watch you," he said and began to enter her faster.

She began touching herself and closed her eyes.

"Look at me Kara," he commanded. He wanted to see her beautiful brown eyes filled with desire as he orgasmed inside of her.

Kara felt as if the galaxy were standing still again. Tir was making-love to her and she could clearly see him, but she also felt like she was watching him on a video com link that had some issues and that he would change. He was still him and she was still her, but they were different. The longer she looked at him the more the other Tir was in focus. "Do you see that," she murmured confused. He was him but a different him and she wanted to call him by a different name.

"I only feel you in the whole galaxy," he barely could focus.

Then he flipped her over like he knew she wanted and began thrusting hard into her.

She lost all thoughts about an alternative timeline at that point as he was going to make her orgasm again. Those ridges and this position, she was in heaven. She didn't care what kind of Alliance magic was at play, she just wanted him so much.

He knew she loved this position by the sounds she was making now. He could feel that he could make her come again if only he could hold on himself. He just about managed.

Then they lay on the bed together for just a short time before Tir picked Kara up and carried her to the shower.

"No, I am not taking an ice-cold shower with you again." She tried to squirm out of his arms, but he just tightened his grip on her.

"You need to take a shower and I want to shower with you."

"How about we turn the water temperature all the way up for me and you can watch and then you can have your shower?"

"How about I get it, so you can turn the water up to 40C or whatever it is you want by tomorrow but that right now you have one last cold shower with me?" He knew that an engineer would have to come and override the safety settings in the bathroom to allow the water to become so warm for her.

She nodded, and they went into the shower together. She screamed again when the ice-cold water hit her.

"I just love it when you do that. That surprised sound."

She ignored him because it was so cold. Soon he was washing her body and everywhere because she could not move. Thankfully they were out of the shower soon and dry. She raced out of the bathroom then to his wardrobe to grab herself the last dress hanging there. It was red. She put it on and then looked for the stockings. "I have no idea where the stockings are, but I want them."

He came up behind her and showed her where they were and

handed her a pair, "You look good in red."

She smiled. "Is it time to eat dinner yet?"

"Soon. We can have some wine beforehand if you want?"

"Yes. I am never going to start a conversation before meal-time ever again unless we are already sitting at the table."

"Good, I will civilize you in no time."

After a couple cups of wine, he wanted to tell her about the slave artist coming after dinner. "I have organized a surprise."

"What kind of a surprise?"

"A slave artist. I want you to understand this part of Alliance culture now that you are an Alliance citizen."

"Was this supposed to be a good surprise or a bad surprise?" She asked thinking this was a pretty bad surprise then reminding herself that he thought she looked good in this ugly, dress with no form whatsoever. But when she thought about the dress again, she was at least happy that it kept her warm and it was comfortable, more comfortable than anything she had ever owned, so maybe it did not matter what it looked like.

"A good surprise. She can recite a myth or an exciting segment from Alliance history."

Kara could tell that Tir was excited by this. She remembered that the Alliance had very little in the form of entertainment and culture, so she looked at him and half-smiled, "I am sure it is going to be fun." She poured herself another cup of wine. "I am not having a threesome with this slave artist though, that is completely out of the question."

"We will see, they can be very convincing, and I know the slave artists are desperate to see a human. You know humans are rumored to be the most beautiful species in the known galaxy."

"And," she stood up and turned around, "What do you think? Are the rumors true?"

Tir took in Kara's lovely form, brown hair, golden skin and pink lips. "I have never seen anyone more beautiful than you are my lovely wife. Especially in that Alliance dress, you are just missing the necklace I gave you."

She frowned and sat down, hoping to avoid having to wear the ornate necklace he gave her to signify their marriage.

"Kara, go and get it. People will think you are ungrateful or strange."

"Or human," she supplied.

He got up then, went into the bedroom and returned with the necklace that she had left in her bag with the dress she had been wearing earlier. He put it on her, "Now you are perfection," he said and kissed the top of her head.

"I thought you said that I was perfection and the goddess herself when I was naked. I would rather be naked than wear this heavy necklace."

"You must become civilized, my human wife. Then you will be able to enjoy everything the Alliance has to offer you and I guarantee you will not be disappointed. Please leave your prejudices behind."

SLAVE

Junior Lieutenant Mux came at exactly eight o'clock and laid out the evening meal for Kara and Tir who had already had more than a couple cups of wine while they waited for the food. Kara had learned her lesson now about meal times in the Alliance and that they were not something to be trifled with.

Mux set down the luke-warm vegetables in front of Kara, "I never thought I would be so delighted to see these texture-less and tasteless vegetables again, but here we are."

Tir sternly looked across the table at Kara, "Be grateful for what the gods provide Kara."

"You know most people in the galaxy eat anytime they want," she said casually. He could not intimidate her. She was a captain of a much lesser starship and had gone into battle against him and others that could have easily just destroyed her if she was not so brave or clever, but not only had she survived she had managed to even get some hits in on him and his other ships. Tir trying to intimidate her now over some food was not going to work at all.

"And who controls most of the galaxy?" he asked condescendingly. "Not any society that cannot control themselves to eat at appropriate times, certainly not humans. It is because the Alliance follows the gods' edicts so closely, we are rewarded in our mortal lives. Do not be so obstinate about becoming civilized, my human wife, it will only annoy us both and it is a battle you will most definitely lose."

Kara wanted to throw a vegetable at him but resisted because she was so hungry. "Listen up my darling Husband," she could see him bristle when she called him that and decided it was better than throwing a vegetable. "I am not a pet that needs to be trained. You forced me to marry you knowing full well that I am human. I am not going to give thanks to any gods for something that I know was procured only by mortal hands. Show me the gods doing something for me and I will give them thanks."

Tir just looked at his adorable human wife then and wondered how he was going to get her to behave in a more dignified manner. Humans really were the most beautiful species in the known galaxy, but they were unorganized, undisciplined, impulsive and heathens. It came as a surprise to him that she did not want to just embrace Alliance culture and thank him for marrying her. When they were intimate things were easy, they had a natural attraction to one another, but when he was trying to instruct her, to civilize her, gain her loyalty, she stubbornly refused almost everything. He had saved her ship and crew, none of them had been harmed, yet she seemed ungrateful. True, he was denying her some things, but it was only because he could not trust her yet. Tir knew though, once she was loyal to him and the Alliance, she would be a strong force to reckon with, not just an annoying bug hanging around the galaxy.

"Kara," he said more gently now hoping that a softer hand might work better, "Do you remember the first time we said each other's names?"

"How could I forget?" she said softly now. They had both felt something larger than them resonate between them. "It was only a few days ago."

"How could you think those feelings could come from anything but the gods?"

"I don't know. Maybe you are drugging me to think so?"

"Drugs are forbidden in the warrior class," he said in a matter fact way that made her curious.

She looked at him confused then and decided to take this further, she needed as much information as she could get about the Alliance and until she could read properly, she had access to nothing but the people around her. "I know so little about Alliance culture. What do you mean, warrior class? I ..." she was interrupted by a chime at the door.

Tir grabbed Kara's hand from across the table and said, "It's someone to teach you more about Alliance culture," he said with a bit of humor that she did not trust. He led Kara to the sofa and then went to open the door.

Kara watched Tir let in the female slave artist. She had not known what to expect as she had never actually seen an Alliance woman more than at a distance or on media, let alone an Alliance prostitute. And Kara had certainly not expected to see the woman who walked in with Tir now.

"Captain Kara, this is slave artist Sera, the most charming woman in the entire Alliance."

Kara did not know if she was charming or not as Sera had not spoken yet, but she could not deny Sera might be the most beautiful creature she had ever seen, despite being grey and wearing an ugly green Alliance dress that looked like a box. Sera did wear a lot of ornate jewelry that added more shape to her dress and now Kara could begin to understand why Alliance women wore the jewelry, to add definition to the boring dresses. Kara was taking in her appearance with fascination. She reckoned Sera must be wearing at least five to eight necklaces all of different lengths and made of different metals with stones as well as many bracelets and long earrings that almost touched her shoulders. She also had her long black hair pulled up in the most intricate braids with many jeweled hair accessories. Finally, Kara looked at her face which was a perfect heart-shape with sharp grey eyes almost matching her skin and high cheekbones and decided that this is what physical perfection looked like. Her skin looked so perfect, that even Kara wanted to reach out and stroke her.

Tir offered Sera a seat and some wine, she took both but only had eyes for Kara. She had never seen a human woman before and was startled by her short brown hair, big brown eyes and golden skin. She wished that Kara had not been dressed in an Alliance dress as it revealed nothing about her figure which had been rumored around the fleet to be so curvy people were saying she looked like the goddess herself. Sera smiled at Kara, "What would you like me to entertain you with this evening?"

Kara took a sip of wine, assuming Tir was going to answer this question, but when he did not answer, she swallowed the wine and asked, "What would you suggest for someone who has been forced into marriage and knows almost next to nothing about Alliance culture? Is there a story about that?"

Sera smiled at Kara and looked to Tir for approval to grant this request. He nodded. "There is the ancient myth about the Lost People I think you would find interesting."

"Is it a long myth?"

Sera smiled, "No it is not long. Would you like me to recite it for you?"

"Yes," said Kara realizing that she had to ask Sera to do something since Tir was no doubt paying her to be there and entertain them. *This is so bizarre,* Kara thought to herself.

Sera stood up then and dramatically began telling the story of the Lost People:

> *Long ago, when the Alliance was still an infant and ships got lost in the galaxy, a fleet of explorers and scientists were pulled to the other side of the galaxy by an unknown force. Unable to come back, they found an almost inhospitable planet, too bright, too hot, but uninhabited except for some small animals. They sent a message back to the Alliance explaining their situation, asking to be rescued. The message took over one-hundred years to arrive. When it was received, the Alliance had already counted those in that fleet dead for a long time. The Empress and Emperor then were very greedy and did not want to waste time and resources to go look for some citizens who may or may not be still alive and waiting to be rescued. The Imperial family decided to conceal the information about the Lost People. They had the message destroyed. From that*

point forward, everything only got better for the Alliance, technology, military, colonies and Alliance civilization in the known galaxy soared and no one thought about the rumored Lost People again, until we discovered a species almost like our own. They called themselves 'humans.' We sent ships to investigate them before they had the technology to understand what we were doing. We believed that these humans were most likely the Lost People. However, since the Empress and Emperor of past had all the original documents destroyed, no one remembers the exact location of the Lost People. So, it was decided, conveniently, that humans were not the Lost People and the Alliance continued to expand and to ignore humanity. But now, the gods are punishing the Alliance for not retrieving the Lost People when we were given the opportunity. They are making us suffer with low-female birth rates and catastrophic disruptions in our perfectly ordered society. We have a choice now, to accept humans back into the fold or die from our pride.

"Who believes this?" asked Kara a bit spellbound.

Sera looked at Tir and then back to Kara, "Any of us who consider themselves to follow the will of the gods."

"So, almost all of you?" Kara asked.

Sera nodded. "Kara, humans are the Lost People."

She shook her head, "No, we aren't. Do you have any proof? Where did all the Alliance technology go then? We have been the last in almost everything in the galaxy. If we were the so-called Lost People we would not be that far behind the Alliance."

"It is possible that they destroyed the Alliance technology to start over. We don't know why or how as there is no record on Earth, although there are many conspiracy theories about it. One thing we all know for certain, humans are the only other species in the galaxy genetically like us and now we have this demographics problem that can only be solved with the integration of human women. It all fits into the story too perfectly.

You have no proof that you are not the Lost People. Nothing you can hold up and say, 'See humans are organic to this planet', because you are not. There are too many similarities, not only in the genetics but in your ancient cultures. You are us."

Kara just drank some more wine thinking about this. She knew so little about Alliance culture and religion so there was no way that she could compare it to ancient Earth cultures and religions.

Sera watched Kara thinking she was so lovely and hoped that she would be able to stay longer, but she had to be invited to do so. "Did you enjoy the myth even if you do not believe in it?"

"It was very interesting as far as myths go, although I honestly cannot believe such a story. I think it makes for good propaganda now though, when you are trying to get human women to have children for you."

"Even if it was just propaganda, do you think it would work?"

"I think the Alliance would have had a better chance if you would have asked us and not insisted on marrying. You are just taking and forcing us to do things that we find barbaric like marriage. Think of all the children that will be born out of anger because of this."

"Will our children be born out of anger Kara?" Tir asked evenly.

"If you continue to keep me on the tight leash you have me on now, then most definitely yes, they will. I am quite used to being as free as you are Tir. And I doubt you would like to be as confined as I am for the foreseeable future."

"This is true, but you are on the losing end of getting what you want. You came to this war probably expecting to die in your little ship." She bristled at him calling her ship little, although it was little compared to his. "Your good little ship," he corrected himself because he didn't think it was nearly as terrible as human technology was always made out to be in the galaxy. "And you didn't die, I saved you but instead of thanks and gratitude for saving you and your crew and even marrying you, you are just trying to escape."

Kara looked at him in disbelief, "And you wouldn't do the same in my position?"

"No, I would accept my new fate and realize that it is a better one."

"Captain Kara," Sera interrupted them, "I have never met a human before. I know little of human culture, could you tell me why you find Admiral Tir so disagreeable? In our culture if someone saves your life, you owe them yours. This is why the Admiral struggles with your stubbornness not to just give yourself to him in every way."

"He definitely has my gratitude," Kara said answering Sera but looking at Tir seriously. "But I cannot just give myself to anyone. Humans do not marry anymore, and we are in control of our own destinies. I cannot just walk away from my beliefs because I got lucky is not something that I am comfortable with. I am not willing to give up my freedom to Tir or mythological gods."

Both Sera and Tir were shaking their heads at her, "The gods control all of our destinies here. You were meant to be with Admiral Tir, you know it Captain. Everyone on this ship can see it between you two but you resist every time you remember something about your life before. Open your eyes and accept your fate."

"Are you a counselor too, Sera? Please stop dissecting my problems. I have been forced into marriage and seen my female crew off for the same fate and just because I don't mind having sex with Tir does not mean we were meant for anything. I have enjoyed sex with a lot of men in my life. It is an animal instinct. There is nothing spiritual about it."

Sera smiled and laughed at Kara's question, "I am far from being a counselor. And, I agree with you, sex is absolutely an instinct all species have, but it does not always stop there. I know that you are clever enough to understand that, even if you do not believe in the gods or fate. Humans must fall in love and even if you do not marry you do decide to spend a considerable amount of time with people you consider special in your life, don't you? I do not know much about humanity but I cannot imagine it being so different than Alliance culture. As far as you and Admiral Tir's relationship, I just am telling you what I know and see. And I can also see that the truth makes you very uncomfortable right now so let's talk about something else. As a slave artist I represent the living and breathing culture of the Alliance onboard. I can tell you anything you would like to know."

Kara looked into her grey eyes, "Tell me how you think my female human crew are faring now on your capital planet being married off like animals?"

"Oh, they would not be just married off. I heard that Admiral Tir pushed you a bit..." Kara interrupted her.

"Coercion," Kara corrected her.

"But I also heard that you had an instant connection, so even if he might have pushed you for marriage, you do not look completely unhappy nor chained here."

Kara had to admit that this was true. Had she met Tir under different circumstances she had no doubt that they would have fallen in love, the marriage part, she was unsure of, but definitely would have fallen in love. "I am not physically chained no, but I am locked in and cannot leave. Who told you we had an instant connection?"

"Someone who witnessed you both together came to see me afterwards."

Kara blushed, she knew that must have been the doctor. She then remembered his eyes on her as she rode Tir. "What did the good doctor say?"

Sera smiled seductively, "He said that your beauty was unparalleled and that your body was the most perfect female form he had ever seen. He was jealous that he could not touch you as Tir was doing, but that he could only be a spectator."

Kara thought about that for a second and she could not help but be aroused. She tried to get control of herself again though before this really did turn into a threesome. "Sera, tell me, how do you think my female crew will find their husbands? Will they be physically forced?"

Sera looked into Kara's eyes and realized she really did not know, "Admiral, you need to take care of your wife and not give the impression we sell women like slaves," she admonished him. "Captain, your female crew will be given lodgings, clothes, food and whatever else they require including an Alliance education. Then they will attend what we call, 'The Assemblies.' At these Assemblies they will have the opportunity to meet eligible men for marriage. As human women are the most beautiful in all the galaxy, and there are so few Alliance women to compete for the men, I think your crew will find themselves with reasonably successful husbands in a very short amount of time and I am sure anyone who doesn't will probably be given reprieve, but I would be surprised if any of them would not want to marry. What else would you like to know about the Alliance?"

"How bad is the demographics issue really?"

Sera looked to Tir then and he nodded, letting her know she could tell Kara the truth, "It is not good. This year we had a seven percent decrease in female babies born and we still do not know why. Our doctors have been working on this problem for over a decade now. The decision to begin taking human wives was not something we took lightly."

"But why would you not just ask us?"

"What if you were to say 'no'. The Alliance could not risk lowly humans telling us 'no'. We have our pride."

"As you all keep reminding me," said Kara looking at Tir. Then Kara had another moment where she felt she had heard this all before, but that it was all different. "Do you feel that?" she asked Tir.

"What do you mean?"

"I feel like I have heard this all before but not just from when you said it earlier."

"I think you are just adjusting to being in a new environment in a new situation."

"I am stressed and there is nothing to do," she said more to herself than to Sera or Tir. "But that is not it, this is more like, I am on the tip of realizing something but then I lose it again. This is the third time this has happened while I am looking at you Tir. The first time was when I said your name and then you felt it too."

"I did, but that was just the gods way of confirming our union."

"Really? Then what are the gods trying to do now, make me feel like I am losing my mind?" She took a deep breath.

"What does it feel like Captain? These episodes you mention?" asked Sera.

"It feels like I have done this before, but things were different like this is a bad dream or the other is a bad dream, but only one is reality and I am stuck in-between without a good connection to either. I have never felt this way before in my life. It only started happening since I came onboard the *Refa*, so you can imagine how suspicious I am about possibly being drugged or something."

"It is possibly a glimpse into a parallel universe," said Sera seriously. "Be careful you don't fall through."

"Impossible," Kara dismissed her suggestion, but looked over at Tir. She could not read his face expression and she wondered what he thought about a parallel universe.

"It is definitely not drugs. Members of the warrior class are not allowed drugs." Sera noticed Kara's confused face and said, "Each class in Alliance culture has made compromises with the others to make sure everyone feels equal. Our warrior class are the highest but also make the most sacrifices in terms of pleasurable activities, no drugs except for wine. But you see I am part of the slave class, I can do what I want when I want."

"You mean you do not have to eat when the gods' decree it?"

"I don't have to, but as a slave, as we are closest to the gods so I always do." Sera wanted to change the conversation, if it stayed this depressing she was never going to be asked back or asked to stay longer. "Has Tir given you any jewelry besides that beautiful necklace?"

Kara instinctively touched the heavy and ornate necklace, "No, should he have? I would have appreciated some kind of weapon more," she said sarcastically.

"I did not expect to get married. This was all I had with me. I have ordered jewelry and clothing befitting my wife that will be on the next supply ship." Then he looked directly at Kara and said, "And some of the human food you like from the one Earth store in the Alliance."

Kara had not expected that. "You bought me some human food?" *Like I am a well-looked after pet,* she thought and then told that thought, *Shut up, if circumstances were different it would be nice, right?*

"Not much. I just got the same as you took from your ship." He wanted her to be as comfortable as possible even though she was still his prisoner because she was also his wife and he wanted to trust her sooner rather than later.

"You know in the Alliance women have lots of jewelry to show their status and complement their beauty."

"It must be something you have to grow up with. I am not accustomed to wearing so much jewelry and I do not like the weight of it. I hope Tir, you don't expect me to wear too much all the time? You have probably guessed already I am happier in a uniform more than a dress."

"I am surprised to hear that. You are such a beautiful woman but without jewelry you only show half of your beauty and half of your status," Sera commented gently.

"Only to Alliance eyes," Kara defended herself.

"Are there any other eyes here?"

Kara said nothing but thought, *I am no doll you are just going to dress up to sit here and have babies.*

Sera stood up and moved to sit next to Kara on the sofa. She looked at Kara's ears and ran her fingers over Kara's pure earlobes and said to Tir, without taking her eyes from Kara's, "She does not even have her ears pierced Tir," then she reached out and took one of Kara's hands and brought it to her own breast and said, "And I doubt a nipple pierced either." She began moving Kara's hand over her dress, enough that she could feel the outline of the elaborate nipple ring she had. "See Captain in the Alliance, we like to decorate ourselves as much as possible. Maybe it is because we all have grey skin? Maybe it is because we are not nearly as curvy as human women? But regardless, we love jewelry and I would say our men like it too."

Kara was surprised Sera had brought her hand to her breast, but she didn't pull her hand away. She was too curious. "Doesn't that hurt?"

Sera was still holding her hand, rubbing it lightly over the fabric of her pierced nipple, "No, it feels good. I have never been so close to a human. I am curious about you. Your hand is so soft and warm," Sera slowly moved closer to Kara and stroked her hair and face. "And your hair and eyes so beautifully brown."

Kara had never had advances made on her from a woman. She did not know how she felt about this. Sera was the most beautiful creature ever, but did she want to do this? She didn't know, but Kara was curious, so she decided that she would let this go just a little bit further and see how it felt. She had to admit, she loved the way Sera's cool, soft hand felt on her skin. And now was curious to see what kind of jewelry she had attached to her nipple now that her fingers had fully explored it.

Sera saw a flash of desire in Kara's eyes and decided to move a bit closer now and she stroked Kara's hair and face again, but instead of stopping at her chin she proceeded down to her neck and the top of her chest. Her fingers just lightly making circles there as she still held Kara's hand against her own nipple. After a couple minutes Sera leaned in ever so slowly, never breaking eye contact with Kara and kissed her. She pulled gently away with Kara's lower lip seductively in her mouth, and then whispered in her ear. "I would love to see what a human woman looks like and tastes like. Would you let me lick you while your husband watches?"

Kara now knew what it was like to pay for sex, but she didn't care, this was so different it was taking her mind off everything else in her life and all she could think was, *Okay, Tir, now I under-stand. It is still wrong though, but now I am just wrong too, but I don't want to say 'no'. I feel so alive right now doing this, this thing that is so wrong, just like marriage, it is so wrong.*

Sera began kissing Kara in earnest then, her hands exploring Kara everywhere. She was so curious about this human. She could feel such curves as she had never felt before through her dress and was tantalizing them both by slowly caressing her body everywhere over the fabric. "So many curves Kara. I am in awe of you already." Then she began putting her hand slowly up Kara's dress, along her stockings which she made sure Tir had a good line of vision for as Alliance men loved these thigh high stockings, even the black every day ones that Kara was wearing now. When Sera got to the top of the stocking, she circled it with her finger leisurely, "Such soft and warm skin. I am going to begin licking you from there, but I want to take your dress off first. Human beauty, let's stand up so I can see you fully."

Sera slowly stood up and guided Kara to do the same and then undressed her with her skillful and seductive hands and lips. Pinching here and kissing there as she slowly took the dress off, pleasuring Kara while at the same time giving Tir a little show. When the dress fell completely to the floor, she took in Kara's body with more kisses and caresses. "The doctor was right, you are just as magnificent as the goddess. It is no wonder that Tir had to marry you and that the doctor was so obsessed he had to have sex with me, imagining you." She sucked on one of Kara's nipples while her other thumb and finger brought the other to a point and after a couple of minutes, switched. Then she worked her way down with her hands and her mouth fol-lowing. "I had heard that humans had hair here, but I had no idea how intoxicating it would look or smell." Sera leaned in and smelled Kara's sex, "May I lick you in front of your husband Kara? Would you like that?" Kara didn't answer her, so she asked again while she ran one cool finger over her vulva lightly, "I think he would like me to lick your legs, thighs and sex while he watched. I think he would like to compare his own performance to mine. Should we give him the chance?"

Kara opened her eyes then and looked at Tir, she had never seen him so aroused as he sat in the chair watching them. She then looked down at Ser who was on her knees before Kara and said, "Sera lick me and show Tir how it is done."

Sera took Kara's hands then and positioned her on the sofa to get a good angle to get at Kara but also for Tir to watch everything. Sera looked back at Tir before she began and licked her lips, "How good does your human wife taste? Will her scent linger on my lips and tongue for the rest of the night?" Sera did not wait for an answer before she turned to Kara and as she promised began licking her inner thighs where her stockings ended.

Kara could not help but jump with the wonderful sensations. She put her hands above her head as she did not want to put her hands in Sera's hair and mess up her elaborate hairstyle. Kara had no idea how many minutes passed while Sera just teased her with her tongue until finally, she settled on her clitoris and then a finger, then, two fingers in her vagina. "You are so wonderfully warm and soft. If I were Tir I would not even be able to show up for duty I would want my penis in you every second. You are so lovely, soft, tight and warm," she said as she moved her fingers expertly in and out of Kara's wet folds. "Kara how am I doing so far, do I compare to your husband?" Sera was consciously saying 'husband' as this kind of thing was a turn-on for Alliance couples, what she did not realize was that it was actually a bit of the opposite for Kara.

"About equal, Tir is good, but I am sure you can do better Sera," Kara said breathlessly with a small smile.

It was not long before she reached her climax and Sera then was just casually caressing her body.

Tir was watching everything completely aroused. He had so many fantasies now about what they were going to do he hesitated for a minute, deciding. He loved watching Kara being pleasured by another woman. Especially now that it felt so wicked as she was his wife and they were aboard his ship. This was something that should not even be allowed to take place with existing Alliance laws but then here they all were because it was war and she was a useful prisoner.

Sera was just licking outside of Kara's vagina entrance again, she could not help herself she was curious about this gorgeous human. "You are so wet Kara. I am glad, I want to taste all of you." With that she surprised Kara by sticking her whole tongue into her vagina suddenly and then continue to go in and out with her tongue.

Kara gasped and put her hands on Sera's head, "I love the feel of your tongue Sera. Don't stop doing that."

Sera continued to use her tongue for many minutes to thrust in and out of Kara. She loved the small sounds of pleasure Kara was making. She pulled back after a suitable amount of time and then began licking her vulva up and down, with big strokes from top to bottom, before she played around her clitoris, finally coming to that special place and so lightly licking it.

Kara felt like she was going to lose her mind. It was not long before Sera had her fingers inside of her again and was bringing her to orgasm saying, "It is so sexy that you are coming in front of your husband again. I am sure he can smell you across the room you are so wet and fragrant. Look at him, he is so aroused waiting for us to finish so that he can have his turn."

Kara looked at Tir through her lustful eyes and said quietly, "Who says we want him to have a turn?"

Sera laughed, "Would you like to punish him Kara? We could?"

Just then Sera was bringing Kara to a whole new level of ecstasy and she forgot to respond. After some minutes, Kara opened her eyes and she had never seen such a great desire reflected in Tir's eyes. Then she closed them again because she felt so good and wanted to just concentrate on the pleasure Sera was still building up again in her. Tir came and picked them both up and carried them to the bed. One woman in each arm.

Once on the bed, Kara began undressing Sera, "I want to see an Alliance woman's body and I want to see how you have adorned your body with jewelry. I want to feel that jewelry against my skin." Kara removed Sera's clothing and was surprised to see a very athletic grey body with pierced nipples and long hanging nipple rings with jewels and a belly-button jewel. Kara was beginning to understand the jewelry now, if you had no curves, jewelry enhanced everything. Kara put her hands on Sera's pierced nipples, "These are beautiful. You are the most beautiful woman in the galaxy." Sera kissed Kara then and their naked bodies were rubbing against each other with desire. Kara's breasts meeting Sera's pierced nipples. Kara loved the cold sharpness of Sera's jewelry against her naked skin. She thought to herself, *This is so different being with a woman and I have never been so aroused in my life with Tir watching everything and the expectation of him inside me afterwards.*

Tir watched for some time again wondering when he was going to join them. After 20 minutes of watching them make out he decided he would participate too. He began taking off his clothing, but Sera noticed immediately and began taking off his trousers and kissing him everywhere and then took off his shirt and jewelry.

Kara could not help but watch Sera undress Tir. She was fascinated that Sera did not do it the awkward way she had done. For starters, Sera had not struggled with the Alliance clasps that were invisible once closed. But even more interesting was that she took off his shirt then the jewelry and she kissed everywhere the jewelry hit before removing it, like she was showing each individual piece of jewelry reverence. It was also so odd to Kara than Sera only kissed his penis and did not take it into her mouth as would have been the natural thing to do if they were all human. Kara had the strong urge to take Tir into her mouth then just to pleasure him in a way that she knew was forbidden, but Tir moved too quickly to achieve what he wanted with both her and Sera once he was naked.

He joined them on the bed and without speaking positioned Sera on her back Kara hovering above her mouth. He was relatively sure Kara would have mixed emotions about him having sex with another woman, even though that other woman would be expertly licking her, but he wanted to watch Sera lick Kara again in this position, he thought it was so sexy.

Kara did not like this new position and frowned at Tir as he kept eye contact with her as he was thrusting into Sera.

Tir wondered how long he could do this before Kara's jealousy took over. And as quickly as they started Kara got up and moved Sera to a seated position and Kara began to get on her hands and knees to lick Sera's sex and enter her with her fingers as she had done to Kara. Sera smelled like exotic flowers to Kara and she was surprised at how cool her skin, even the inside of her vagina felt, so alien and strange. Kara loved licking Sera while her rear was up in front of Tir. He was playfully caressing her anus and vagina. Kara finally took a break, turned her head around and said, "Tir please."

He loved watching her lick Sera, he did not want to hurry things. Tir thought Kara was so adorable as she turned around and begged him to enter her then that he could not deny her. He positioned himself and entered her vagina slowly and she moaned a bit from the pleasure of him inside of her. His hands were on her hips as he moved back and forth and then grinding into her. He was holding eye contact with Sera. He wanted to tell her how jealous Kara was, but he assumed she already had figured it out. He loved being inside of his warm human. He was thrusting faster and faster and even though he did not want to come yet, he could not help himself.

They all lay together afterwards on the bed for many minutes, and then Sera quietly excused herself. After she was gone, Kara said, "You are never allowed to put your penis inside her ever again."

Tir smiled but Kara could not see it. He put his arm around her and pulled her close, "But I am so glad you are still calling this a 'forced marriage' Kara."

Kara did not know if she could ever get the image of him having sex with Sera out of her mind and it almost made her physically ill. She didn't know why. She had never considered herself a jealous person. And she knew she was not in love with him, but some serious lust she guessed. "If we have to be married, which obviously we do because I can do nothing about it, then I don't want your penis in anyone else. I think that is how humans used to behave within a marriage in the past and I can see why now. You are supposed to be mine, forced marriage or not."

"I enjoyed watching you and Sera together, I thought you might feel the same," he hazarded.

"No, I didn't. I only felt jealous," she admitted quietly.

He ran a hand through her short hair and felt touched for this strange emotion she was having over a slave artist. "I will not have sex with Sera as long as you say you do not want me to." That was the best compromise he was going to give her right now.

After a couple minutes of just lying in each other's arms on the bed, Kara got up then and went to one of her bags from her ship that she was supposed to have unpacked but hadn't and pulled out some of her favorite pajamas and put them on.

"What are those?"

"Pajamas."

"Stop," he sat up then and noticed a small bloody scratch across her breast, he gently touched it.

She looked down and said, "It must have been one of Sera's piercings that cut me." And went to put her pajama top on.

He stopped her and looked at it again and then kissed it. "We must make sure it does not scar."

"What? You are kidding me right? That will not scar. Now let me put on my pajamas."

"Some cuts can leave small scars; your skin should be perfect except for aesthetic piercings of course if you want."

"No, I don't think I would ever want that. And I am sure my skin will be fine." She tried to put on her pajamas again and he stopped her.

"We don't wear night clothes, they are unhealthy remember?"

"Yes," she sighed, left the clothes on the floor and then just got into bed to get warm. She had gotten very cold without any clothes on and felt like she was sobering up a little, she just wanted to be warm and sleep now.

Tir paid Sera by touching his fingerprints to a tab on his desk and turned off the lights and got into bed with Kara. Neither one said anything about the day that seemed like it had lasted a lot longer than 24 hours.

An alarm went off in the middle of the night. Tir jumped up put on a uniform and was gone in less than a minute. He hardly had time to say, "We are under attack," before running out the door.

Kara got up and got dressed too. She definitely was not going to stay in bed while they were being attacked in case this might be her opportunity to do something or to escape. She looked for her uniform everywhere but could not find it, so in the end, she had to put on the same dress that she had worn the day before. Once she was dressed and her hair combed, she approached the door and opened it. She had learned half of the hieroglyphics to read decently in Alliance now and had memorized the door code by watching Tir put the code into the door. The door slid open and the two guards were there.

The guards looked at Kara with a bit of surprise that she had opened the door. She hoped they might believe Tir had given her the code, "I was going to go help," she lied and before she could say where, they were shaking their heads and one guard pulled his sword out to threaten her.

"No, you are not. Go back in. I will lock this door from the outside. You will only get food when Admiral Tir returns."

Kara did not move so the guard with the sword moved in front of her and pushed her back into the room with the sword, hard enough that she fell to the ground. When she rose, the door was now locked from the outside. *Oh well*, she thought, *She had to try. If they were in the middle of a battle, then there was a chance there would have been no one there.* She went to go sit on the bed. She had the shades lifted to see if she could see any of the battle, but she could only see very little.

After watching for about 20 minutes all the ships had changed positions now, including the *Refa* and she could see much more of the battle raging outside. Tir was sending out his fighters now. She wondered which formation he would use as she knew from last time their two usual formations were terrible against the Jahay who's fighters were faster and were able to maneuver around the larger more powerful Alliance fighters. When Kara saw that Tir was making the same mistake she wanted to tell him not to, but then she hoped that this was just a ploy and they were doing something new, but no, after five minutes she saw he was just sending pilots needlessly to their deaths because he had obviously had not come up with a new plan yet as this was a surprise attack and he had been busy having sex with her instead of doing his job. She thought about it, he of course would still win with this tactic only because the Alliance outnumbered the Jahay but it was wasteful. She knew she should not feel the least bit guilty, but she could not help it, he had been pleasuring her instead of working. She went to his computer and sent him a new flight plan and she knew it was so easy that all he needed to do was send it to his pilots.

Tir was on the bridge watching his pilots die wishing he would have been more prepared for this battle when he received Kara's message. He looked at it and then copied it and sent it out to his pilots. Of course, it was brilliant, so simple but so brilliant and she made it all up hungover watching from his bedroom window. *Gods,* he thought, *Don't ever let us be equally matched and her not be on my side.*

Kara watched now to see a change and after 30 minutes her plan was being implemented. The Jahay unsure of what was happening did not know how to respond. Half of the fighters thought the Alliance was falling back and the other half were falling back themselves just as Kara had predicted. It was not long before the Alliance fighters had the upper hand and were destroying all the Jahay fighters before they could return to their ship. The battle was over 20 minutes after that.

But it was not until ten hours later that Tir returned to their quarters. He found Kara asleep at the dining room table which he thought was a bit strange. "Kara," he said gently as he came up behind her and lifted her up into his arms.

"Wait no, the food. I am waiting for some food," she said half asleep.

He stroked her hair, "Did you try to leave?"

She nodded against his chest.

"I will order you some food only because you helped me win that battle today, which I was very grateful for."

"I figured it was partly my fault you were so unprepared, and I did not want our sex life to slow down because of it," she admitted.

"I will go against the gods and get you some food. I am sorry about the orders, but Kara, you are still my prisoner, so you cannot leave." He did not need to ask her how she opened the locked door, he summarized that with her new studies of their written language she had probably easily memorized his code.

He ordered her food and then sat with her in his arms on the sofa. She was not sleeping but she was very tired and just lay against him with her eyes closed. "What have you been doing all day after the battle?"

"Studying, waiting for you. Waiting for food." Then she mentally turned off her translator to see if she could understand what he said next.

"What chapter are you on now?"

She was elated she could understand him, but she did not want to risk speaking back and it being wrong now, so she spoke in English as he would not even guess she had turned off her translator. "Chapter 34. Almost halfway."

"That is good. Soon you will be able to read almost everything, so I will have to be even more vigilant." *Gods,* he thought, *She is too clever. She must get pregnant, then gods' willing, her loyalty to me will be certain.*

She turned her translator back on, she had understood most of what he said so she was pleased with herself given that she had only begun a couple days ago and recognized less than 300 words. Thankfully Alliance grammar was not very difficult. She lay her head against his chest then as he stroked her hair. She thought, *Enjoy this while you can Rainer because you are going to leave as soon as you can.* But then that same voice inside her head said, *The more you do this the more difficult it will be to leave. You are playing with fire.* She told her mind to shush then and she just peacefully tried to think of nothing but the pleasure of being held by him and his strong hand stroking her hair.

After many minutes the door chimed, and Mux came in with food which he laid out in the dining room. Kara sprang up and into the dining room to eat without saying anything to Mux or Tir, she was so hungry. She had not eaten for over 24 hours. She did not even care that it was the same boring vegetables, she ate them as if they were delicious, which they definitely were not.

After she finished, Tir led her into the bedroom where he took off her dress and put her to bed and did the same for himself. He pulled her close in the bed. His head was resting on top of hers, "There will be one more battle I reckon," he said softly.

"I think two major battles are left," she countered him. "The Jahay will draw this out for as long as possible. Wouldn't it be better to hunt them down? You have this massive fleet."

"I am waiting to meet up with two more fleets here." He was confident she had no access to communications and could not relay that to anyone. "Then they will come to us. We are more powerful. We do not need to chase them down. We have the resources to wait. And," he grabbed her breast and began pulling gently on her nipple, "The sooner the war is over, the sooner I have to send you away."

She put his hand over her breast to urge him on more. Her thinking was that the sooner she became pregnant the sooner she could gain his loyalty stay on ship and escape. She knew if she were left on the capital planet, she would never escape. His other hand was caressing her vulva and the top of her thighs now. She enjoyed how he got her to orgasm quickly sometimes just as much as when he did it slowly on purpose. Kara knew he was tired now but appreciated that he was not going to orgasm if she didn't or at least he gave it a really good try. She reflected that he was beginning to know her body better than she did herself and made it perform for him. It was not long before he was making her come with his fingers lightly tapping her clitoris on intervals with descending circular strokes. She was grinding her hips back into his hips and groin and could feel his erect penis on the back of her thigh just waiting its turn. She came so hard that he had to hold her in place to finish and once she had he was gently pushing his ridged penis into her, holding her close from behind, his hands on her breasts.

The feel of him going in and out of her slowly from this angle was almost too much. She reached back with one of her hands and put it in his long, thick hair and pulled him down for a kiss. Afterwards he moved his hands to her hips and began moving more in earnest. He knew she wanted him to enter her, 'like a dog' as she had said once before but he really wanted to see her now. So, he flipped her on her back and put her ankles together, resting on one of his shoulders as he began pounding into her. He loved the way her breasts moved with each thrust. And the way her cheeks were flushed with pink. It was only minutes before he found his climax and then lay beside her and pulled her close again and the blanket over them.

Kara slept comfortably with the enemy. Her thoughts as she drifted to sleep were, *You really have done it now. You have married, slept with a prostitute and now helped win a battle against your allies. You are a traitor Kara Rainer.* But even though she knew the truth and the person she was one week ago would be upset with her now, she could not be that upset with herself having had to make the decisions that she had had to make about her crew, their lives and her current position. *Nothing in life was ever clean*, she thought and then drifted off to sleep with her hand resting gently on Tir's waist.

In the morning, they were awakened by Mux bringing in breakfast. They got up and ate silently. Afterwards Tir said, "I have to go. You must stay here. Learn the hieroglyphics and there are some children's books there you can try to read too.

I might be gone a long time. Do not try to escape or else the guards will not feed you as you discovered yesterday."

Kara was not looking forward to a day alone again. "Can you send Doctor John here for the midday meal? I usually eat with him. I will be lonely here all alone again."

"No Kara, he is working with Siu. If you get really lonely, call for Sera or another slave artist to entertain you."

"I am not going to do that," she said but as soon as she said it, she thought she might actually do just that. The thought of her and Sera alone without the interference of Tir, but then she thought she was so hypocritical saying he could not sleep with her when that is exactly what she wanted to do suddenly.

"Your thoughts are clear across your face Wife. Fortunately for you, I am not nearly as jealous, and you can have your fun with Sera. I do not mind, just don't make it a habit, she is very expensive."

Kara blushed, "We will see."

Tir got up then and left.

Kara went to the console and began studying. Well after the evening meal she had become so bored and lonely, she opened Tir's computer and called Sera. She was not really in the mood for sex anymore as she had been that morning but rather just someone to talk to.

When Sera arrived, Kara explained, "It is just me. I have been locked in this room all day yesterday and today. I am lonely."

"I can imagine," Sera said sympathetically. "Would you like to hear a story or do something else?" She smiled sweetly at Kara and innocently touched her arm.

"I would like to talk to you actually. I know almost nothing about the Alliance and Tir is not really forthcoming with information."

"What would you like to know about specifically? Do you mind if I sit?" Sera asked.

"Let's begin with the classes, you and Tir have both mentioned it but I do not understand."

"In the Alliance, we have three classes, the warrior class,

which is what Tir is, the merchant class, there are none onboard, and the slave class which I am apart of and about a hundred others onboard. Every Alliance citizen then belongs to a symbolic house no matter what class they belong to. In that house, they are born into a role or job with very few chances to make choices for their futures themselves."

"What about Tir?"

"He was born into an imperial family, which there are two. It has always been expected that he would join the military and become at the very least a general. It was not unexpected though that he became an admiral as he is a very good leader and then because of this and that the exchange of imperial families is near, he has been chosen to be the Emperor's successor. You know this right?"

Kara nodded, "Yes, he mentioned it. But I do not understand how that works."

"Every couple hundred years the Empress and Emperor retire and choose who will lead next from the best of the imperial families. Usually a new Emperor is chosen, and he will marry a suitable woman and they will rule together until it is their time to retire and choose someone else to take their place."

"But Tir has not chosen someone suitable, has he?"

"No," said Sera honestly. "But he has chosen you for religious reasons as he believes humans are the Lost People and he is making an example out of himself."

"How many people are religious like he is? That believe we are the Lost People, I mean."

"Many people believe and many more don't say for fear of being ridiculed, but if Tir were to bring you back with a child and take the throne I think there would be some unrest but that in the end, he would succeed."

"Or be killed and me too and whatever offspring."

"We never kill children."

"That is reassuring," said Kara sarcastically.

Sera gave her a disapproving look and then said, "But I am sure Tir is going to do his best and make excuses to keep you out here for as long as possible before the exchange. His fleet is loyal to him and no matter what they may personally feel about him marrying you, they would never let any harm come to you or sell you to the highest bidder of abductors."

"People want to abduct me to get to him?"

"Yes, to prove a point that religion might not be real, that he is not as strong as he thinks he is marrying a human and getting away with it."

"Wait what? I thought humans were supposed to be Alliance citizens now? I have just sent my female crew on the word of Tir they would be treated well there. Now what are you saying?"

"They will be treated well there, but Tir is supposed to be Emperor. No one wants him marrying a lowly human, no matter how beautiful, no offense." Kara showed she didn't care with her hand and nodded for Sera to continue, "Humans are meant to be for lower-ranking warriors who could not find an Alliance wife."

It was all becoming clearer now why he was adamant that she also memorize some religious prayers to say in public. He told her she need not believe but she just gives the appearance of believing. "What do you think? Are we the Lost People?"

"Without a doubt and I think Tir is right in marrying you. You will see."

"Is there anyone else to take his place so that he can just remain in the military?"

"There are some others, but they are much lower than he is in the military and the Empress does not like them as she likes Tir. It is a problem. It is the Empress who wants you to disappear now."

"What do you think he wants to do?"

"I don't know. You know I just speculate. He has never shared any of his private thoughts about anything with me."

"Thank you for being so candid."

"This is common knowledge Kara, you don't mind if I call you that as we have been intimate?"

"Kara is fine. Since we have been intimate I want to know about intimate things in the Alliance," Kara smiled at Sera, "Tell me now about periods. Doctor Siu mentioned a thing called 'the tab'?"

"Yes, it is a tiny machine that used to be shaped like a tab on clothing, but now it is the size of a very small line of three balls and they go into your vagina and take care of all the blood and alleviate the pain until the end of your bleeding and then they come out."

"Does it fall to the floor? You don't wear underwear."

"Underwear is unhealthy. No, it just waits for you to take it from the entrance to your vagina. You will see." Then she looked over at Tir's small shrine and said, "Or maybe not. Tir has the fertility goddess front and center. I would say he wants you to get pregnant as soon as possible."

"Yes, he does. But I don't think anything is going to happen as soon as he would like. It has been a mess with the war, stress, low food rations, you can imagine."

Sera looked at her then and asked, "What do human women do for their periods?" She always so curious about other species, but especially now about humans as they were genetically the same.

"We have a little cup and it catches the blood."

"Oh, that sounds…"

"It is not nearly as bad as it sounds."

"I am sure it is. No offense but I don't think anyone in the galaxy understands humanity's desire to 'remain close to nature' as you call it."

"We have no religion but a strong culture that focuses on the connection between us and our planet. It is difficult to explain to off-worlders. Tell me about yourself Sera. How is it that you came to be on the *Refa*?"

"I simply made arrangements to come onboard when Admiral Tir took command."

"Have you known the Admiral for a long time?"

"No, only for about one year." Sera was enjoying the look on

Kara's face, she could not decide which would win over, jealousy or curiosity.

"And how well do you know him?"

"Well, I know him by reputation of course and personally I have met him privately twice and that includes yesterday."

"What kind of reputation does he have?"

"Religious, honorable and efficient," Sera could see that these things did not seem to mean much to Kara, so she continued, "He believes in the Alliance and will do anything, even marry a human, to see it survive."

"Do you really think bringing in human women is going to help boost your female birth rates?"

"I am no doctor," Sera laughed, "but we must try something." Then she paused and continued conspiratorially, "I know that it was always planned from the onset of this war that human women would be taken back to the capital as a trial."

"A trial to see if it biologically works?"

"No, we already know that it will biologically work. This is a trial to see if Alliance citizens would accept human females in society. There were other options, like polygamy."

Kara laughed, "So men like Tir would rather have a human wife than have to share with another man?"

Sera smiled, "Admiral Tir was so against polygamy he spoke in the High Council for human women, this was all his idea actually, to take you during the war. He said that military women would be emotionally stronger and more open-minded than a human that has never left Earth."

"Yes, that is probably true in some ways," she did not want to mention that a lot of the women she knew who would probably like to be married to an Alliance man were are all still on Earth, she did not want to give any of them any ideas about just taking more human women. "But what do you think his long-term plan is with us?"

"I think to just show that human women, if willing, can adapt and serve as a stopgap to fortify the Alliance civilization against further decay, until we figure out why less and less females are being born."

"I wish I could get word to my people about this so that we could have some negotiation points, if that is even possible, before you begin just taking us. Maybe to appeal to the Alliance's moral side of this. It is not right to force us into it."

Sera shrugged, "It is tough being bullied, but if I can say anything for the Alliance, most of us do believe that you are the Lost People, so you will be treated with as much respect as we can give you. This is why you are here married to Admiral Tir and not chained up to a medical bed as they do fertility experiments on you."

"I don't even want to ask if the Alliance has done that to other species."

"No, because you know we have. We do not rule the galaxy by being nice."

"I know, it is just the image you just put in my head was terrible."

"Because it is a terrible thing, but the galaxy can be that way, you of all people must know that? Life cannot be easy for humans, always being the last." Sera paused taking in Kara's sad expression, "Have you told your family the good news?"

"What good news?" Kara was bewildered.

"That you are married to Admiral Tir."

Kara laughed, "I would not call that good news. Humans don't marry anymore, we see it as an archaic practice that has no place in the modern world. They would be horrified. I am assuming my first officer will let my parents know what happened. Tir of course only allows me access to internal communications onboard ship and to access the children's learning programs so I can learn to read."

Sera smiled, "And I am sure learning our spoken language too. I have heard that humans like languages of the galaxy and you can turn your translators on and off." When Sera saw that she had guessed correctly she said, "Don't trouble yourself, it is nothing to me. I also use every opportunity I can to make my situation more favorable. Can you say something in Alliance? I want to hear what it would sound like."

Kara looked at her and said seriously, "Chapter one, first hieroglyphic," in what she hoped was acceptable Alliance to be understood.

Sera smiled at her, "Totally useful in every day conversation."

"Did it sound clear, nothing came out as nonsense?" If the translators could not translate something it was registered as gibberish. Kara turned her translator back on then.

"Totally clear but with a slight accent of course. So strange to hear an accent." Sera looked at her and then said, "Say this, 'I am human. My name is Kara.'"

"I am ... My name is Kara," she struggled with the unfamiliar sounds.

"Human," Sera said, and Kara repeated the word about six times and then was able to say both sentences correctly. "Gods, you are so adorable," she then said to herself more than to Kara. "Don't let Admiral Tir know, he will become more obsessed with you than he already is if he hears you speaking with that accent."

"'Obsessed' is a strong word."

"That is what everyone is saying. He almost messed up yesterday, which is something he has never done, and it is because of you."

"But he didn't mess it up in the end."

"No, but ..." Sera trailed off. "I think he is struggling with wanting to be with you all the time and introduce you to our ways, to show to everyone that he is correct and that it works with a human, but then at the same time, remembering as well that we are in the middle of a war. And he knows that one of these things, either you or the war, will have to wait, as he cannot focus all of his attention on both at the same time, which is what he wants to do. Or rather focus all of his attention on you," she smiled. "And I do not blame him," she said suggestively.

Kara blushed remembering what they had done sexually the last time she met Sera.

Sera rose and took Kara's hand and guided her back to the bedroom as she said, "You are a prisoner here, you might as well just enjoy some of the benefits of always being so close to a bedroom with not much else to do." Kara resisted a bit and then Sera kissed her, quite expertly and said quietly in her ear, "I will teach you to speak Alliance like a native if you teach me how to love a human. We both need these things. What do you say?" Sera asked as her hand was already up Kara's dress caressing her sex.

Kara turned to kiss Sera as her answer.

ESCAPE

Kara looked at Tir across the dining table, "Is that all you are going to say?" She had been alone all day and was desperate for some conversation.

"I'm not going to share classified information with you. When the Jahay lose this war, which they undoubtedly will, Earth will pay reparations with the rest of the Jahay allies. I'm not going into any details about it."

Kara frowned. She was exasperated with her monotonous existence as a prisoner on her husband's ship. Every day was almost the same. She was confined to his quarters without any communication off-ship. In the mornings, she studied both the Alliance spoken and written language and she frequently practiced speaking Alliance with the smart mirror in the bathroom. In the afternoons, she would try and break into her husband's computer to access outside communication or anything that might aid in her escape. Escape was constantly on her mind. Sometimes she was allowed to meet her own doctor, John, the only other human onboard, for the midday meal in the mess hall, but that rarely happened anymore after she tried to run away from her guards and succeeded for about ten minutes to allude them. Ten minutes is a long time to be gone on an Alliance Starship. Occasionally when she was very lonely, she would ask Sera, the slave artist, aka prostitute, to visit. But Kara tried to limit those intimate visits to once a week, because the shame of paying for someone to see you was exhausting as well.

"I am going crazy here. Am I your wife or prisoner? You must choose."

"If I could trust you, you would not be confined to my quarters, but every time I have given you a bit of freedom you have proved that you have no loyalty to me. I saved you Kara. I saved your ship and crew. I have not treated you unjustly. If you were me, would you let me roam around your ship in the middle of a war?" he asked.

"I would never be in your position. I would never keep a prisoner-wife-husband-whatever, you know what I mean, in the first place."

"And you honestly cannot imagine a scenario where you would have rescued me, and we would have fallen in love?"

"I am not in love with you," she said defiantly. "This is lust." She looked into his green eyes and then said, "And if I would have rescued you and we fell in love, then you would not want to escape. You would follow me to Earth, and we'd live there forever."

"I like your confidence, that I would just give up everything to live on a little insignificant planet on the edge of the galaxy. I like this fantasy, tell me more about our human home," he said softly.

"It wouldn't be cold and muted like here, human homes are warm and colorful, and we can eat when we want. We can do what we want anytime."

"It is unfair to compare life on a ship in the middle of a war to your home during peace."

She ignored him because she suspected that life on any of the Alliance planets would not be too different from life on his ship, organized, unbending and predictable. "I have the sweetest little apartment we would live in, with a yellow kitchen that has a balcony that overlooks a busy street below where the trams go by. I love the sound of the bell the tram makes before leaving the stop. In the early mornings in summer, I open those balcony doors and drink my coffee and watch the people go by and I am so happy then." She looked up at him and he seemed genuinely interested so she continued, "In my sitting room, there is a sofa which I made myself from a patchwork or old fabrics with different patterns and needlework. I am not an artist, but both of my parents are, so I do like to create things sometimes. In the bedroom I have a four-poster bed that has been in my family for a long time. It hardly fits in my room, but I like it. I have curtains on it because the light can be so bright in the summer mornings and I'd rather have three heavy curtains on the bed than on my beautiful windows where I just have curtains for show."

"It sounds very old-fashioned for a starship captain."

Kara shrugged, "Humans value beauty over all else and some of the most beautiful things were created centuries ago. What is your home like on the capital planet? I am assuming that is where you are from?"

He nodded, "It is modern and functional. As you probably know, in the Alliance, most art, with the exception of religious pieces or jewelry, is considered frivolous. We use the colors of our planet in all homes, grey, yellow and black. Some more modern people have begun painting a room red here and there, but that is considered almost scandalous."

"Do you have a red room in your home?"

"No, but I have a feeling if I sent you there, you would paint the whole thing red."

She laughed, "But you are not going to send me there, are you?"

"I don't want to, but you need to accept your new life. I know that you can feel that this is your destiny, why do you resist?"

"Tir, destiny does not exist. We all control our own fates. We are at war, as stupid as that is for humans to be, and I have an obligation to my people, just as you do to yours. Why don't you just let me go and then after the war, let's see?"

"Do you ever wonder in a different timeline if that is how it would have been? Maybe that we met and married under different circumstances."

"Sometimes," she admitted. "But this is the situation now and I want to go."

"I understand that, but I can't let you go and even if I did, your own people would accuse you of being a spy." He didn't think actually think she realized that, she was young and still very idealistic.

"No, they would know you coerced me into marrying you and I was kept a prisoner."

"No, they would not believe you. This is your future now."

"I can't accept that," she said very determinedly.

"There is a story, I will not tell it to you in its entirety now but the gist of it is that all people used to be have four arms and legs, but we so angered the gods they split us in two as punishment and so now we are always looking for our other half," he paused making sure she was listening. "When you have what we have, you have been one of the rare people in the world to find your other true half. Whether it is fate, or we have been blessed by the gods, I do not know, but you are my true half Kara. I know you feel it too."

He moved his hand to touch hers and she did feel more at peace, she could not deny that. Nor that humans had a very similar story written by Plato, but she did not want to encourage him further in his Lost People fervor, so she said nothing.

"Every day I want this war to end, but the same time continue forever so that I can keep you here with me and hope that you start to accept your destiny. However, I know it is a risk because every day, you learn more and are that much closer to escape. And if you do manage to escape you may die, by my enemies' hands or your people's and then whatever our true destiny is will be passed on to others." He looked at her seriously, "Kara, I want to live out our destiny."

She didn't like it when he was so serious like this about things she just could not believe, it scared her, because she was worried, she might just start believing him. She was quiet for a couple minutes and then said, "I don't like the way you keep me locked away in your quarters. I need exercise. I need to get out and do something else. If you want me to start believing that this is destiny, you need to begin to treat me better."

"Now you are being somewhat unreasonable. I have tried to give you some freedoms and you have tried to escape. As for exercise, the only exercise we do onboard is swordplay, but there is no woman to teach you and women are not allowed, no that is not what I mean, it is just that there has never been a woman here, women have their own places." It was difficult for him to explain his culture to her and he always felt that he was completely inarticulate and only made it more confusing.

"I don't care, let a man teach me then." Kara realized she had said something wrong because Tir looked scandalized.

"You don't understand in the Alliance, men and women are not equal in the way that one role can be substituted for another. Everything is prescribed. A man could not teach you. It would go ..." Kara interrupted him then.

"Go against the gods, I know," she looked at him then and tried to look desperate. "You are my husband, we are as close as two people can be. Surely, you can teach me how to use a sword. How can that go against the gods? Even the gods must understand that this is an extreme and unique circumstance." She was looking at him thinking, *Please do this for me. I am so bored all day every day and I am going to become the woman in the yellow wallpaper if something doesn't change.*

Tir thought about what Kara had requested for a couple of minutes, weighing out the pros and cons, "I will teach you. You must learn at some point anyway and I can hardly bring a female teacher onboard especially when we are still at war."

"One more battle and it will be over, especially now that Admiral Uikoly of the Jahay is gone."

"Thanks to you," he wanted to give her credit where it was due. She had privately helped him strategize before the last battle and it was because of her this war would soon be over. He was constantly impressed with her intelligence but that also made him wary of giving her too many freedoms onboard because he worried about her escaping before she realized that they were meant to be together.

She nodded. She had mixed emotions about what she had done, and she had hoped he would have given her more freedom after she handed the Jahay to him in the last battle. "I have always had to be creative or else I would be dead. I would have thought you would have given me a bit more freedom after the last battle. That I could at least meet John regularly for the midday meal."

He ignored her suggestion as they had had that discussion many times. He changed the subject completely then, "How are your studies of Alliance hieroglyphs going?" He got out his communicator as he asked her the question and wrote a couple sentences and then showed it to her. This was a game they played frequently.

Kara looked at the sentences and knew all the words but two, but read out the sentences in English anyway,

> Every day I am more amazed by your intelligence. Now let's go to the ... and practice ... which is something that I am good at.

She looked up at him, "I don't know those two words," she pointed them to the small screen.

"Gym and swordplay," he replied. He was amazed at the speed she had conquered the Alliance written language and he thought, *Because they are the Lost People, it resonates with her to learn the language the gods gave to us.* And then another thought occurred to him, *Have humans been learning other languages in the galaxy because they are still looking for their true language, Alliance?* Humans were the only species in the galaxy that had the ability to turn their universal translators on and off. The rest of the galaxy laughed at them for this, 'Why in all the stars name would you want that?' people always asked, but he looked at Kara now and wondered if this was why.

Kara was beaming now at the thought of getting out and doing something new and something physical. She had not left his quarters in days. She got up from the table and said, "Let me change my clothes," and went into the other room to put on her yoga clothes, tight black pants and a pink tank top. She did not even care that she was going to be cold in such little clothing on the Alliance ship which was kept at a cool 15C. He had acquiesced to keep his quarters at 19C for her.

When she walked out into the sitting room he took in her appearance, "Good." Then he opened the door and escorted her to the officers' gym which was busy with half-naked grey officers. As they walked along the side, everyone stopped and saluted Tir. He acknowledged them and walked on with Kara behind him to a smaller room in the back. They went in. He began looking around the room for something.

Kara just stood near the entrance and watched him. She suspected this must be a room for him alone. "Who do you usually practice with here?"

"Doctor Siu, he is the best in the Alliance," Tir said casually.

"How do you know he is the best?"

He looked at her and smiled, "Because we have frequent competitions in the Alliance."

"How do you rank?"

"Not well enough that I would enter a competition, but I am standing here so I have yet to lose a duel".

"And women?"

"They also have competitions, but they are not for male spectators," then he came over and handed her a heavy blunt sword. "Only women can compete and only women and male slave artists can watch."

"Male slave artists? That is strange."

"It is rumored that a male slave artist for a year is the prize in the women's competition, but only women know if that is true. It is forbidden to talk about these things with any man, even your husband."

"What is the men's prize?" *Alliance culture is so messed up*, she thought as she asked the question.

"Only the honor of winning."

She looked down at the sword and asked, "A practice sword?" As she tested it, she commented, "It's a little heavy."

"It is a man's practice sword, for obvious reasons there is not a woman's one onboard. But the weight difference is only a couple kilos, I am sure you can manage. You are strong and in good physical condition. Hopefully, this will come naturally to you." He watched her investigating the sword. He found her appearance now completely tantalizing.

She was just looking at the sword, wondering what it was composed of to look so brown and matt, when Tir suddenly came over and had his tongue in her mouth so sensually, she almost dropped the sword. She thought to herself, *Surprisingly, a worn yoga outfit and practice sword is obviously a big turn-on for an Alliance man.* His hands began to roam then, and she pushed him back a little, "Tir, we can do that later, right now I want to do something new. Teach me."

He looked at her swollen lips and ran his thumb over them, "You are right, but later. There is so much about you right now that is forbidden and I cannot begin to explain it, but you will understand in time. All I can tell you is that you look irresistible to me, but I will do my best to teach you without becoming too distracted. Let's begin now." Tir took off his shirt and put it to the side so now he looked the same as all his officers that they had passed on the way in. He quickly braided his long black hair in a perfect braid down his back and she wondered then how many times in his life he had done that. He walked into the middle of the room with a practice sword for himself and she followed. Then they stood across from each other, looking at each other eye to eye with no emotion for about half a minute. Kara thought to herself, *And now you look enticing to me, but I will not be taken in by your charms when I have the chance to do something new.* Just then, Kara had the feeling then again that she had done this with him before and she tried to shake it. She did not want to say anything because he would tell her it was the work of the gods and honestly, she just wanted to do something that was not having sex, talking about religion, learning Alliance or thinking about escape. So, she ignored the feeling and tried to focus.

"Have you ever fought with a weapon like this before?" he asked her seriously.

"No, I am from the 25th century."

He frowned at her, "Be serious Kara. We often resolve personal conflict by the sword. You are an Alliance citizen now and you will be expected to do the same."

"Fine. I am sorry I made fun of your culture, again. I hope cheating is allowed?"

He was still looking at her quite seriously, "It is not only allowed but expected. You will be dead if you attempt to follow some sense of honor. It's funny you should ask that though, it never occurred to me that humans even knew what rules or honor were."

She smiled at him, "Oh, we know the word, 'rule', we just don't care. It is difficult to think about rules and honor when you are the most disadvantaged civilization in the galaxy."

"I wouldn't know," he admitted. For centuries the Alliance had controlled the galaxy and Tir never considered how less powerful civilizations felt about compromising their morals to just maintain independence. He began instructing her then, beginning with how to stand and gave her some tips on simple movements. "Now I want you to move forward like this," he showed her, and she did it well for someone who had never held a sword before.

While she was practicing the simplest movements and stances she asked, "How many duels have you been in Tir?"

"Five."

She waited for him to continue and was annoyed that he didn't, "And all of these were to the death?"

"Yes."

"Before me, had you ever talked to an off-worlder before?"

"Of course, I have, many times. Why would you ask me that?"

"Because whenever I ask you a question you answer me as if I should already know."

He thought about this for a minute and she hit him hard with her sword in his stomach while he was thinking. He looked at her with a feigned disapproving look, "All I can say in my defense is that you are the first person I have ever met who does not know all of this about me already or know about Alliance culture in the first place. I am not used to talking or having to explain either." Then he looked at her seriously and said, "I have been in five duels to the death. Four were to protect my place as successor to the Emperor."

"And the other one?"

"It was a private matter."

"I am your wife," she couldn't believe she was using that again to get him to do something for her. *Who am I? I am your wife*, she smiled to herself at how absurd and barbaric it was. Then could not control her mind and thought, *That's me, I am a wife barbarian with a sword now.*

"My sister was courting a man who treated her inappropriately. There were other options open to punish him, but he chose a duel. This, you must never speak of this to anyone."

"But surely people wondered why he died?"

"In the Alliance people die and we don't always know why."

Kara was shocked be his admission, she had always imagined the Alliance to be a place of transparency and rules that were followed. "And my female crew, what if they just die?"

"You have my word that nothing will happen to them. I am not explaining this well. Don't be anxious, your crew is in no danger. We have very little crime in the Alliance and the little crime we do have is all very personal. Women are treasured above all else in the Alliance. Your female crew are quite safe."

"You are not assuring me with that answer."

He struck her lightly with his practice sword, "I apologize but I can't explain it any more than that. You must trust me. Now, let's focus on this."

Kara brought her sword up again and resumed the same

movements as before thinking about how vicious the Alliance must be that they legitimately solve issues through dueling to the death.

After an hour of practicing movements and techniques she was beginning to falter, "I must stop now Tir or else I will not be able to pick anything up tomorrow with this hand."

He stepped forward, took the practice sword out of her hand and then put them both on the floor. Then he took her right wrist up to his mouth and lightly kissed it while he looked into her beautiful brown eyes.

Kara found him so attractive now with his shirt off and his hair pulled back as she had never seen it. She leaned into him as he kissed her wrist. She could see the desire in his green eyes and wondered if they could have sex here in his little private gym. His guards were not outside this door and the door was not locked as far as she knew. She could still hear a lot of his men practicing outside. But she had to admit, she liked the excitement that any of them could walk in on them at any moment.

Tir pulled slightly away from her and was looking into her eyes deciding what to do. A part of him wanted to take her now, but the door wasn't locked and if he took the time to do that it might ruin this moment and he wanted to live out this fantasy. It was forbidden in the Alliance for men and women to spar together. Even more, to be in the same gymnasium. Her being here was one of the most popular fantasies played out with slave artists in the Alliance. But what made this even sexier for him was that this was real. She was here, dressed in athletic clothing and he saw her holding a sword for an hour. It was just too sexy, he finally decided, and he just could not help himself.

Kara reasoned that it was doubtful any of his men would walk in and if they did, it would not be too shocking that they were having sex. As far as she understood from Sera, his crew were talking about their sex life anyway. Sera had told her it was mainly because she was human, and everyone was wondering if she really was going to become pregnant with a hybrid child.

Tir was running his hands over her pink top now. He was making her nipples hard and he was aroused by how they looked through the fabric of her shirt. After some minutes, he moved on to groping her breasts over her shirt while standing behind her. She was leaning back into him and he thought, *Yes, we are definitely going to do this.* After many minutes of touching her breasts over the fabric, he then put his hands into her shirt to touch her breasts skin to skin. Now he knew that she was past any point of saying 'let's not do this here.' She was grinding her hips against him and he began attempting to remove her shirt, but after some futile attempts, he could not figure it out, there did not seem to be any buttons or clasps. So, he just scooped her breasts up, so they were held out into the open air with her shirt pulled down, just begging to be sucked. At this angle, he almost thought they looked bigger and fuller, which he found so sexy. He moved in front of her and began licking, sucking, lightly followed by a little bit of biting and pinching. She was making the most wonderful little sounds as a reaction. As he was still sucking on one her breasts, he moved his hand down to caress her sex over her tight pants. "You are so wet already," then he slowly took down her pants and began kissing and sucking all around her stomach, thighs and vulva. Then he made her turn around with her pants still around her knees, "Bend over Kara," and began licking her rear and all around her anus.

Kara had never had a man lick her there before and she jumped from the sensation. The next thing she felt was Tir holding her steady by her thighs and then a smack on her bottom with one of his hands. She smiled with the sensation and could not help but say, "Please punish me Tir. I have been such a bad human."

Tir smiled and thought, *My wife has more fantasies than I do apparently.* "Tell me what you have done."

Kara thought quickly about what would annoy him and tried to list them all, "I was disrespectful about the eating times," he smacked her once and she paused to see if there would be more and there wasn't so then she tried to think of something worse. "I was disrespectful about your culture," he smacked her a couple times then, but she wanted more. "I tried to get past the safeguards on your computer," he smacked her a good ten times for that, and she was starting to feel really good then.

His finger was lightly circling her anus waiting for her to say something more. He knew she was enjoying this new sensation. He knew about the computer and of course it had come as no surprise to him that she had tried. "Is there anything else?"

Kara was trying to think, she felt his tone changed, did he know something real and was waiting for her to confess? She didn't know, she had been alone too much she could not read people anymore. She must have been quiet for a minute because he hit her again, this time it was harder and then asked the question again. "I have had sex with Sera without you and didn't tell you."

Tir rubbed her bottom then and said, "I know you have done that. There are guards at our door." He knew she wanted more but he was not going to give her what she wanted until she confessed more. "I can use the practice sword to make you tell me how you have been naughty."

Yes, do that, she thought excitedly. "Oh no, not that," she said a bit over dramatically.

Tir had to really try to not laugh then and thought to himself, *She could never be a slave artist, she is a terrible liar.* He reached over and picked up one of the heavy swords and stood next to her. She was still bent over with her yoga pants around her knees. He took the sword and rubbed the width of it against her rear.

Kara felt the cold sword slide against her bottom and became so aroused with anticipation. Then, without warning he spanked her with it, and she felt the tingling everywhere.

"What else have you done to deserve this my human wife?"

Kara had completely forgotten she was supposed to think of some other things, her mind was blank with both pleasure and pain. "I had a fantasy about the doctor and masturbated to it."

He was silent then, she did not know if she had crossed a line or not. She still did not fully understand how sex and monogamy were perceived in the Alliance.

Tir was surprised by what she had just said, and it took him a minute to decide if she were telling the truth or lying. In the end, he decided that she was probably telling the truth. So, he smacked her hard with the sword a couple times. "Do you wish he would have joined us on our wedding night?"

"Yes," she replied.

He smacked her again a couple times and then put the sword down and rubbed her red bottom. He kissed it and licked her anus. "Would you like the doctor to put his penis in here? The place you told me I could never go."

His tongue was in her anus now. It was such an unusual but good sensation, she thought for a minute that maybe she did want to try that with someone. *If the doctor hurt me, he could probably fix me afterwards,* she thought and then replied, "Yes, I want you both inside of me at the same time."

"You are so naughty telling me before you never wanted to do that," he said but he did not spank her again he just continued licking her, now he was moving her down to lay on her stomach while he began licking her vulva and vagina from the back and he had a finger in her anus. "We will have to stretch this out you know?"

Kara did not say anything, there were too many new and pleasurable sensations going on. She loved the feel of her breasts against the cold floor and his hands, fingers and mouth on her most vulnerable areas while she lay with her pants around her knees. Soon he was making her climax and then seconds later he had his trousers down and was pounding into her. He held her by her hair then and pulled on it a bit roughly. "Yes, Tir. I am so bad."

Tir loved the feel of thrusting into her like this, he needed her to say something she may not understand but it didn't matter, "Say 'We shouldn't be here.'"

"We shouldn't be here. It is forbidden. It goes against the

gods," she smiled to herself thinking, *See I have learned a lot of things from you.* She was rewarded by him turning her over then and pushing her legs down to one side as he began pumping into her roughly and one of his hands pinching her nipples. "This is so forbidden," she said quietly for good measure even though she had no idea what was so forbidden, she thought having sex on the conference room table was much naughtier than this. Then a thought occurred to her, if they were being super naughty, she wanted to bring it to the next level for him while he was in the mood to go against the gods. She pushed him back and quickly began sucking on his penis before he could pull her off. She tasted herself on him and she reflected that she had never done this with any man.

Tir had only had slave artist lick and suck his penis before. Kara was so different as it was so wrong in this place and as she was not pregnant yet, but it felt so good, her mouth was so much warmer than an Alliance woman, he could not resist her. He had his hands in her short brown hair, with the intention to push her back, but it felt too good, he just ended up with his hands firmly in her soft hair while she pleasured him with her hot mouth. He was going to come soon. He said as much to her, hoping she would stop but she didn't she just continued, increasing her speed and pressure until he started to come and then she was perfect, not letting go but her mouth became so gentle guiding the semen out into her mouth. *Gods, I am going to die now, it is too good.*

Kara swallowed all of his semen which tasted exactly the same as human men's and she wondered then if they were the Lost People. She smiled to herself, *Seriously Rainer, after all the other thoughts you have had about the subject, the taste of his semen is what sways you? Classy.* Kara got up to her feet, pulling his trousers up as she went and then her own. She looked into Tir's face with a devious grin, "Later you can punish me for that too."

"Don't worry. I will," he said as he tried to adjust her breasts back inside her shirt for her. Then he walked over and put on his own shirt. "Let's go. We can come back tomorrow."

Kara followed him out the door, there were less men practicing there now. The all stopped and gave Tir the respect he commanded, and he acknowledged them and then they walked on. Kara wondered how many of them had heard them inside Tir's private room. It made her aroused again just thinking about it.

When they reached his quarters and went in, she said, "I am going to have a shower alone." She wanted to have a hot shower now and think about everything. "Just tell me one thing, why was it so bad to have sex in the gym?"

"Women have their own areas and as I said before men and women never practice with each other. Moreover, we are on a starship, Alliance women rarely leave the planet, let alone would go into that particular room on a starship. It was so forbidden, and I loved it."

"Even my mouth sucking all the semen from your penis," she asked as innocently as she could, and he could not help but smile at her feigned innocence.

"Don't remind me Kara, it was all so wrong. We cannot do that again until you are pregnant. It goes against the gods."

She shook her head in disbelief and thought, *I am so tired of hearing that.* Then she took off her clothes and went into the bathroom. She sat down on the toilet and the toilet adjusted itself for her height, species and for her specifically. Then she got into the warm shower. Tir had had the engineers take off the safety setting so she could have a much warmer shower than what any Alliance citizen could go into without being burned and she was grateful. She stood under the water for some time constantly telling the shower that she was not done yet when it reminded her that she had been under the water for too long and it would dry out her skin. Finally, when she got out of the shower, the mirror, her good friend the mirror, greeted her.

"Good evening Kara. You are healthy today. Now all you need is a good night's rest."

"Thank you mirror."

Kara went out into the bedroom accompanied by a cloud of

steam the size of the bathroom door and found Tir already in bed probably asleep. She put on her stockings and nothing else, as she liked to sleep with socks on. And she especially liked the stockings Alliance women wore under their dresses as they were even better, warmer and softer than any human socks or stockings she had ever worn. Even more, they went all the way up to her thighs and never fell down. So, she put them on and then got in bed and drifted off to sleep comfortably, thinking all the while, *When I escape, I am taking all these pairs of stockings with me.*

In the morning, Tir woke up at his usual time and looked over at Kara asleep. He touched her hair gently before he got out of bed. While he was getting dressed, he looked at her and he realized that she was wearing her stockings in bed, as one of her feet was sticking out from under the covers. He smiled as he went over and ran his hands up the stocking until he reached her thigh, then he pinched her.

"Oww," she said and opened her eyes, "What are you doing?"

He then playfully grabbed the top of one of her stockings and began pulling it down slowly. "Why are you wearing these in bed?"

"I like having something on my feet at night and I must admit these stockings are divine."

He took her other leg and removed the second stocking. "It is unhealthy Kara and I find it a little unhygienic as well."

"Says the man who has no problem having sex all around his ship."

"That is different," he defended himself.

She shrugged her shoulders, grabbed the blanket and turned back over to sleep.

"Kara," he said while he touched one of her shoulders. "It is breakfast soon. If you miss it, you will be hungry."

She didn't move, "I am not hungry. I am just tired. Eat without me."

"That is bad luck. Come on. Get up then you can go back to sleep."

"No, I don't care about food this morning. I really am tired. I think I am sick. Please let me sleep."

Tir left Kara in the bedroom but was very concerned for her. He wondered if she had caught an Alliance flu, it was going around. He ate breakfast and checked on her again before he left, and she was sound asleep. He went by sickbay on his way to the bridge. Doctor Siu was involved in a private procedure with a patient, so he could not talk with him. But the human, Doctor John, was there and since this was about Kara, he asked him, "Captain Kara was so tired this morning she did not want to eat breakfast. I think she may be ill."

John tried to look the Admiral in the eye and not smile at his overprotective attitude. He had noticed that Alliance men talked about women as if they were so fragile and mysterious, he wondered how they ever managed any kind of equality in their civilization. He might have found ese tendencies endearing if they were speaking about children or pets, but not adult women, "Does she have any other symptoms besides being tired?"

"She said she was not hungry, and she just wanted to sleep."

"Maybe she just wanted to sleep?" John was just trying to be the voice of reason. "My captain would say if she were unwell."

"I don't know how long you served with your Captain, but she never misses a meal and she is never that tired. Although, yesterday she had a lot of exercise," he noticed the doctor's surprised face expression and clarified, "I was teaching her how to use a sword."

"Maybe she has her period? That can make some women tired. I am sure it is nothing serious. I can go and talk to her later if you will allow me?"

"Yes, as long as you take an assistant with you and then report back to me what is wrong with her."

John agreed and then watched the Admiral go thinking, *I wonder what life is like for Captain Rainer with him taking such extreme care of her all the time? She might prefer to be alone in the brig rather than all his attention.* John had not seen Kara in weeks because the Admiral did not want her roaming around the ship and escaping. So, he only knew of Kara's current condition through the rumors circulating around the ship about her and the Admiral's sex life and threesomes with the slave Sera. He did not know whether to believe the rumors or not. He assumed that Captain Rainer was doing whatever she thought she needed to do to try and escape, even if that meant having threesomes with these grey aliens. He was not one to judge. He was quite contently working in the Alliance sickbay.

John was a prisoner of sorts too, but his invisible chains were to the sickbay and learning about Alliance medicine, which he welcomed as it was much more advanced that human medicine. In return, he was sharing information about human medicine, which was much more organic based. It seemed to him as well that the Alliance doctors were mainly only interested in human fertility. He was surprised at first when he learned that the doctors onboard had never studied any aspect of fertility and that they were denied access to most medicine and procedures that involved only women. When he questioned this, Siu replied, 'On our planets, doctors are all women. Men are only allowed to be doctors aboard starships and on colonies. When we are at home, women doctors treat us all.' John was surprised by such a professional separation between the sexes, but he just accepted it as another major cultural difference between humans and Alliance citizens.

Hours later, Kara woke up and still felt tired. She figured it was all the sword practice yesterday. She rallied herself to get up and dressed so she would not miss the midday meal. She told herself she only had to do one chapter of hieroglyphics and then she could go back to bed. She had just left the bedroom when Mux came in with her food and said, "Doctor John will be visiting you after the meal."

She smiled at this news. After she finished eating, which she did faster than she usually did with the expectation of meeting

John, she just waited for him in the sitting room. She waited only about 10 minutes before John and an Alliance medical assistant came to the door.

"John," she said excitedly. "It is good to see you." She just nodded to the assistant. "I assume you are here officially?"

"Admiral Tir was worried for your health as you missed breakfast."

She laughed a little, "I was just tired."

"I am sure that is all it is, but I have to check because he is so concerned, like you are a beloved doll." John was taking her figure in now that he had not seen her in weeks, but it was impossible to discern anything under the Alliance women's fashion for dresses with no definition.

He took out a small medical device and held it over her as he talked, "How have you been? I heard you really have been a prisoner here in the Admiral's quarters. I have tried to come and see you, but obviously I have never been allowed. I guess they thought I would be colluding with another prisoner."

"Yes, Tir is suspicious about everything" She sighted, "I have been as well as can be expected. I have been learning Alliance hieroglyphics to pass the time." She wanted to say so much more but the assistant was there spying on them.

"I am sure you are way ahead of me as I only know the ones on the medical equipment so far," Kara interrupted him.

"Bravo doctor, Bravo."

He looked at her and knew immediately by her expression she was very upset by something. Bravo was something used to signal an emergency or maybe she meant it to mean something urgent. But he needed to keep talking as not to raise suspicion from the assistant, "Interestingly, I have been sharing a lot of information about human women's fertility. I honestly think they are never going to solve their problem with less and less Alliance women being born. I just hope that whatever is infecting Alliance women does not spread to the human women that have been taken to the capital planet. I believe it is something in the environment."

"What about Alliance women living off-planet?"

"You're joking right?"

"No."

"Alliance women, except for slave artists, don't leave planet if they are of child-bearing years except under extreme circumstances. And slave artists are forbidden to have children if they have chosen that as their profession."

"Well, all of that is terrible."

"I know," said John and he wanted to ask her about Sera and the threesome but held his tongue in case it wasn't true. No matter what their situation now, he was still her captain.

"I didn't realize that Alliance women were so put upon. I thought they were more equal like on Earth. I hear conflicting things from Tir."

"I don't know," said John. "It is strange because some things for men seem totally skewed the other way." He stopped scanning her then and asked, "Kara, you are six weeks pregnant, did you know you were pregnant?" He wondered if that was what the 'Bravo' was about, aborting the child.

"No. I don't feel pregnant. I think you must be mistaken. I can't be," she was genuinely shocked.

He showed her his scan and said flatly, "Congratulations." John looked into Kara's eyes and they both knew that this was trouble. He had thought, like Kara, that even though Alliance citizens and humans were genetically compatible in theory, the thought of mixing two species without heavy medical intervention was impossible.

Kara immediately touched her abdomen, "Is it a little monster? Mixing species like this?" Images from horror movies popped into her mind of deranged doctors mixing species. Aliens creating hybrid monsters.

"It is not a beast, it is only a baby."

Kara was listening to all of this. Of course, she knew this is exactly what Tir wanted to achieve. To show that humans really were the Lost People and that it was the gods' will that humans be integrated back into their society. But she felt a bit of betrayal at providing this for him, for even welcoming his touch, as it may mean the extinction of humans. There are so few of them and so many Alliance citizens and too few Alliance women.

"I feel sick," she said and got up and went to the toilet to throw up. She was sick from the idea of being pregnant with a hybrid child and what that would mean to all the religious fanatics in the Alliance. When she finished, she splashed some cold water on her face.

"You are dehydrated Kara, you should drink some water."

"Why didn't you tell me I was pregnant, Mirror? I thought we were friends," she said sarcastically.

"Pregnancy is not within my parameters. Only men serve on starships."

Kara sighed and went back in to sit on the sofa across from John. "Tell me now what happens? How much longer until it is born?"

"You don't know?"

"Why would I ask you if I knew? What do I know about babies? I was never thinking of having a child. I don't want to be a mother." She had ended her last relationship with a man named Micah because she didn't want to sacrifice her career for a family. She never thought she would be able to become pregnant with Tir. Her menstrual cycle had been crazy this past year and he was a different species, *Wasn't he?* She noticed his assistant looking at her in shock and reminded herself to curb her comments.

"Gestation in humans is 40 weeks and 45 for Alliance citizens. I reckon we should aim for about 42. Otherwise you don't need to do anything differently as you are hardly doing anything now. Just try not to become too stressed about the situation."

She gave him a scathing look, "Sure, I am going to have an alien's baby on an alien ship that might just be the greenlight to overtake humanity based on Alliance religious zealousness, but you are tell me that I should not get stressed out about it?"

"Kara," he put his hand on her knee, "I don't think this is going to be the greenlight to destroy humanity. Remember these people are still quite racist. None of our female crew has even married on the capital planet yet. And they have all told me that they are fine."

"You've spoken to them? When?"

"About two weeks ago. They wanted to speak with you, but the Admiral would not allow them."

"Typical."

"He allowed them to speak to me for medical reasons."

"Good."

"And they were all absolutely fine. They are living in a little guarded apartment-type building in the capital with teachers that come in daily."

"Teachers for what?"

"I don't remember exactly, nothing out of the ordinary, culture, reading, you can imagine. They were told that they would be back in space again, but with the Alliance Fleet. The High Council has apparently allowed human women the right to maintain their jobs on starships if they want, even though apparently, all human women are now considered Alliance women."

"How can they do that? You would think the Galaxy Court would do something. We didn't ask for this nor do we want it."

"I guess they can because no one can tell the Alliance 'no'. The best we can hope for is that they abandon this plan and sort their demographics issue another way. First as to not destroy human civilization and second, because humans won't solve the issue, it is something in their environment, of that I am almost sure of, but it must be so close to them, their daily lives, they are not even considering it," John was lost in thought then.

"Well me being pregnant is not helping in the hopes they will give human women up, quite the opposite," she frowned. "I am worried about my female crew. It is not right what the Alliance is doing."

"I agree, but there is little we can do here and now."

Kara felt guilty then because she could do more, she could submit and possibly gain some influence with Tir to get her people home. Or she could kill herself and the hybrid child growing inside of her to show that human women would not be subjected like this. "It would be better if they just took us by force, I think than trying to marry us and integrate us in this strange manner. At least then we would know what we were fighting against."

"Maybe the Alliance is not as terrible as we are imagining them to be?" John suggested.

"I don't know," Kara answered, "I feel this is all a test to see how docile we are or something."

They were all quiet for a minute and then John gave her a hypo-spray of some vitamins, "Eat well and take it easy, Captain."

When John returned to sickbay, he decided to tell Admiral Tir about the pregnancy in person. He contacted the Admiral through the ship's internal communications and asked him for a couple of minutes privately.

Tir was waiting for him in the conference room, "Captain Rainer," John began, but Tir interrupted him.

"Captain Kara, she is married to me now and we rarely use our surnames."

"Captain Kara is pregnant. Both are healthy. She should be monitored though as this is the first hybrid."

"Good," the Admiral said and then dismissed John. He would speak to Siu later about the details. He now needed to decide what to do with Kara. He wanted her to stay with him, but it was unheard of for a pregnant woman to be on a starship in the middle of a war. However, sending her back to the capital planet was not necessarily the best idea either given his enemies would use her against him if they could.

Just as John was leaving the Admiral called him back.

"Do human doctors know about female bodies?"

"Yes."

"Do you know how babies are born? What I mean is, would you be able to help Captain Kara deliver this baby here?"

"Of course, Admiral."

"Fine," then he dismissed the human doctor and thought, *This changes everything now. I can keep her here, safe, close to me and prove to everyone the gods' want us to bring humans back into the fold.*

After a couple of hours, Kara went to the internal communications and called Sera to come and see her. Within 10 minutes Sera entered and Kara told her about the pregnancy.

Sera looked at Kara seriously, "The gods have blessed you."

Kara just looked at Sera and said nothing. She did not feel blessed. She felt scared for what ramifications this may have for humans. She didn't want to think about it. She wanted to just be with Sera now, like a drug.

Sera picked up on her feelings, "But you've not called me here as a friend today or for the deal we made? You have called me here professionally."

"I have called you here to make me forget what I have just learned. To take my thoughts away from myself."

Sera stood up and took Kara's warm hands without saying anything and led her into the bedroom. Once there, she quietly began undressing Kara. Her cool soft hands tenderly taking off her dress and lingering here and there all over her shoulders, arms and torso indiscriminately. "Turn off your translator Kara. I want you to hear me in my own language as I touch you."

Kara nodded and mentally turned off her translator.

Sera slowly pulled Kara's dress down to her hips and then stopped, edging her fingers around her soft, warm waist. "I also can't believe that you have a child here. There is hardly any sign. You still look so firm, but there is still a long way to go." Then her hands rose to her breasts, holding them gently, "But I should have noticed these, they are bigger I think." She kissed one and looked up at Kara making eye contact. "How could you have not noticed? They are more sensitive too," she said as she blew on her wet nipple and it became very hard.

Kara felt she was in a different world when Sera was touching her body and speaking to her in Alliance. It was so different being with Sera, trying to comprehend a new language and a new kind of sexual partner all at once, she couldn't think of anything else but the present when they were together. "I don't wear undergarments with this dress. I thought my breasts hurt because why."

Sera smiled at her bad grammar, "I understand, my beauty," Sera began massaging her breasts very gently then and lightly licking and kissing them. "Alliance women would kill to have a body like yours. You are truly blessed."

Kara put her hands down to Sera's face and brought her up for a kiss, but Sera stopped her.

"You must ask me."

"Kiss me," she asked, and Sera obliged. She adored Kara's accent on Alliance and this secret that only they shared, that Kara could speak as well as read. She also adored just being with Kara. It had been a year since she had been with a woman regularly and she enjoyed a woman's touch as much as a man's because it was so different. Sera liked to have variety, which she had missed being aboard a warship with only men. She began running her fingers through Kara's hair while they kissed, cupping the back of her head. She felt Kara's warm hands taking off her green slave clothing and even she was anticipating their lovemaking.

Kara's mouth moved away from Sera's mouth and found one of her earlobes. She tenderly touched the long, ornate earring with her hand and kissed her ear then whispered, "I love all your embellishments. They are so exotic." She then began kissing her way down her neck, past many necklaces to one of her breasts that was also pierced, and a long piece of jewelry hang exquisitely from the nipple. She kissed the nipple, as she had done her ear lobe and put her hand on the jewelry, tugging just a little to bring a ripple of pleasure and pain through Sera. Then she put her mouth on her breast and licked her nipple.

Sera wondered if she was addicted to Kara's warm mouth. It was amazing the difference a couple degrees made. Kara's hot mouth and then the cold air brought a new level of oral sensations to Sera's skin.

Kara began kissing her again and then Sera pulled off the rest of her dress, falling to her knees. She brought her hands up both of Kara's stocking legs, stopping where the stockings ended on her upper thighs. She ran her fingers around the top of the stockings, looking up at Kara, who was looking down, watching her. Then she moved one of her hands over Kara's vulva and pulled a bit on the brown hair there. "I love your hair here. It is so exotic. Never remove it." Sera was running her fingers through her nether hair enjoying the look of increased desire in Kara's eyes. Then she moved her hands back to the tops of her stockings and said, "I remember you don't want me to pull these down as you get cold," she said kissing all around her inner thighs, around the top of the stockings. Sera then moved to begin licking all around Kara's vulva.

Kara could feel herself becoming so wet in anticipation with what Sera was going to do. This was exactly what she needed, this pleasure and to be with someone who had no say in her decision or future. Just someone to give her pleasure.

Sera finally moved to licking Kara's clitoris and then moved to put her tongue in her vagina as she continued to stroke her sex. It was not long until she was bringing Kara to climax and then cooling her down with slow light strokes across her vulva, admiring the hair that had become wet from her arousal. Sera looked up at Kara then, "Your cheeks are so pink."

Kara looked into Sera's grey eyes, "I know you like that."

"There is so much I like about humans," Sera said as Kara guided her onto her back and began kissing her down her body as she talked. "I love your patches of hair, your warmth, your different colors," then Kara reached her clitoris directly and Sera gasped and put her hands on Kara's head, "And your hot tongues. Yes, right there. You are so naughty going in and then leaving," Kara had begun licking her elsewhere, "teasing my clitoris like that."

"I know you like it," Kara then urged her to turn over on her stomach and began licking her vagina, first just skimming the outside but then thrust her tongue in and out with her hands on her bottom, spreading her. Again, Kara thought she tasted like some kind of exotic flower, not like a human woman at all, not that Kara had any experience with human women beyond herself, but she knew what she tasted like and then she wondered if this were some slave artist thing. Something they purposely did to make themselves smell and taste like flowers.

"Will you to put your fingers inside of me?" Sera asked.

Kara put one finger inside of her vagina and moved it slowly in and out, looking for the sensitive area that would bring Sera a blended orgasm. When she found it, she had Sera move her hips up and had one hand on her clitoris and the other going in and out of her to give her as much pleasure as possible. "Do you like my fingers on your Alliance skin?"

"In my Alliance vagina," she corrected Kara and then she orgasmed. Kara let her hands gently moving for a minute, then retracted them to move up and to lie next to Sera. Kara caressed her beautiful grey body lightly and casually as they lay next to one another on Tir's bed.

Sera kissed Kara and then held her while she stroked her soft human hair. "Tir will be back soon."

"Yes," Kara said reluctantly.

Then Sera disentangled herself from Kara and got out of the bed and put her clothes back on. "He won't want to see me here when he arrives, not today." She looked at Kara and felt pity for her, she did not believe in the gods and felt she was betraying her people by doing this. "Kara, the gods give each one of us free will. Make a decision."

Kara just nodded. She knew what Sera meant. She must decide about her life and the baby's life.

Sera kissed her on the forehead as she lay naked on the bed and then left.

Tir entered sickbay and Siu led him into his office to speak privately. Siu began, "You should send her to the capital planet."

"I have thought about it and I want to keep her onboard. It is too dangerous at home. People will use her against me. I have also spoken to the human doctor and he says he can oversee the birth."

"This is unprecedented, men watching a birth. People will say we have lost our minds and what if she or the baby dies? It is too risky."

"They won't die. This is meant to be. She is healthy, and their doctor is knowledgeable, right? You have been working next to him for months now."

"Yes, I believe him when he says he can do something."

"It is settled then. She will remain here. We will keep this all as secret as possible until the baby is born. I worry about my enemies wanting to prove that humans are not the Lost People by separating Kara from me and killing her, the child or both."

Siu nodded, "I understand, she could not be anywhere that is safer than on our ship right now. My only concern is her health, an Alliance baby has never been born off-planet before, I worry we are tempting the fates."

"Or maybe the gods are trying to show us the way forward. We must keep our eyes open."

Tir went directly to his quarters from sickbay and found Kara in the sitting room studying hieroglyphics. He did not interrupt her but sat down next to her while she finished. He loved watching her concentrate on something, he found her serious demeanor intoxicating, the way her big eyes focused on understanding the problem in front of her. She looked the same when she was strategizing battles.

Kara closed the program, "I assume John told you I am pregnant."

He looked in her eyes and asked, "Are you not the least bit

excited by this news?"

"If it was just about us," she pointed between them, "then maybe I would be. But this is about you and a myth that you have somehow turned into a law to subjugate human women for your own purposes."

"This is about us too. You cannot pretend to be so emotionally cut off from me or us. We are destined for each other," he took her in his arms. "And this is about the future of both our civilizations, we are one species," he said quietly. "This is the gods' will whether humans believe it or not. I believe and I will make this happen to save us all."

Kara wanted to say, 'But humans were doing just fine without you,' but she couldn't, because the truth was that they weren't. They were barely hanging on to their own independence year after year. They weren't strong enough yet to protect themselves in a galaxy that was filled with civilizations bent on conquering as much territory as possible. And humans were thousands of years behind technologically in the galaxy. Human technology was the running joke of most other species. The only thing that had kept them safe was their obscure location in the galaxy, but those days were coming to an end. Humanity needed a new defense. She knew that Tir recognized this and that is why he believed he was saving humans too. However, Kara like most humans, given the choice, would rather die than enter into an outrageous partnership focused on hybrid children with the Alliance.

"We must go to the public shrine onboard and thank the gods for this blessing. Do you remember the prayer?" Tir asked her.

"I am not doing that."

"Kara, stop acting like a child."

Kara did not respond to that. She decided she didn't care actually. She went to the bedroom and got the necklace, put it on and then they walked out of his quarters.

She walked behind him through the corridors to the main shrine. It was a small room with very little decoration, but some white statues of what Kara assumed were the Alliance gods lined up perfectly in the front of the room and along the walls. There was a large candle burning at one end of the room and the smell of incense burning from somewhere else in the room Kara couldn't see. There were a few other people there that looked up when Tir and Kara entered, but no one saluted him as they had done in other areas of the ship.

Tir pushed Kara forward and nodded at her. She dutifully said the short prayer he had made her memorize to the goddess of fertility, who she assumed she was standing in front of, and then he did the same and went to go light a candle. After a couple minutes of silence, they left. They did not speak to each other on the way back.

Once in his quarters he went directly to his own shrine and kneeled before it lighting a candle. She sat on the sofa and watched him. She wanted to be respectful, but she just could not believe that he would have faith in religion, something humans had given up years before.

Tir finished praying and sat across from her, "I want you to be seen in the shrine every day giving thanks to the gods."

"Only if I get to go by myself," she did not expect him to grant this request, but she had to try.

"No, the guards will of course follow you."

She reckoned that was still better than nothing. "Is there any particular time of day I should be doing this?" All she could think about was medieval women having nothing better to do than go to church and pray as an activity during their days.

"An hour before the midday meal."

"Anything else?" she asked with a sharp tone. He didn't answer her and looked deep in thought. After a few minutes she asked, "What are you thinking about? You look so severe. I thought this is all that you wanted?"

"It is, but now I am concerned about keeping you safe and this a secret until the baby is born."

"Are there many onboard who would like to harm me?"

"A few I imagine but my guards are good and loyal. This is a dangerous time. Everything, I have worked for will fall if anything happens to you now."

"We have nothing to worry about except me going crazy from boredom."

"Kara, I know you like to make light of serious situations, but please, not now. I don't want you doing much or seeing anyone, not even Sera, until the baby is born."

"That is a bit overprotective don't you think? Sera is one of the only people you let me talk to. You cannot deny me her visits."

"We cannot risk anything right now. Sera can be bought as many people can be. I will be more than pleased to grant all the freedoms of an Alliance wife once you are holding a healthy baby in your arms and have proven yourself loyal."

"I want a translator," Kara recognized she had some bargaining power now.

"After the baby is born, I promise you an Alliance translator."

"I want to have communication with my female crew that you sent to the capital planet."

"Limited, but I will allow it in good time."

"I want a ship."

"I am not even sure I can trust you to walk down to the shrine and back. I am certainly not giving you a ship."

"What can I do to change your mind? I would have an Alliance crew loyal to you, it is not as if I could get far. I could be a big help in the final battle."

"I am trying to keep you safe. You are definitely not going into battle only to find an easier way to escape. I may not be as intelligent as you are Wife, but I am certainly not a fool either."

"I want to talk with my crew that you sent to the capital planet as soon as possible."

"I know you already have had an update from your doctor, so there is no rush."

She looked at him and again wondered what he was hiding. "What difference does it make?"

"I will decide when you can talk to them. Not tomorrow or the next day." He didn't want her telling them too much about her life onboard or that she was pregnant. The Alliance needed to believe she was here by choice and that they were destined to be together.

She decided by his tone that there was no way she was going to find out why she could not speak to them tomorrow. She needed to put him in a better mood for him to explain his reasoning, so she dropped it for now.

She switched back on her hieroglyphics learning program and began the next chapter. He went out again and did not say where he was going. He did this sometimes and she did not ask, because he always was back within an hour, usually less. She assumed maybe he had more work to do or was talking to someone, a friend possibly.

After the evening meal, she went to him and put her arms around his neck. Seductively she said, "You still haven't punished me for last night, as you said you would."

He kissed her and then said, "No, but now that will have to wait. I don't want to do anything that might hurt the baby."

"Just a little, I don't think it will hurt the baby. I know you have that whip in your wardrobe."

"Kara, no." He was so aroused thinking about what happened at the gym and how he could whip her now for it but then he thought about the baby and used all his self-control to separate himself from her physically.

"So, we are not going to even have sex? People don't stop having sex when they become pregnant Tir."

"This is too important."

She came up behind him again and put her arms around him. He sighed and put his hands over hers, "Tir, I need you. I am so lost right now, and I need you. You are making me betray my people and I don't believe in the gods' or destiny. It is just us, just you. I need you to make me believe this is right or I honestly don't know what I will do." *I might kill myself or the child*, she thought.

He turned around and kissed her. In between kisses, he said, "You have me." He put his hands on the sides of her head and looked into her brown eyes, "You are saving everyone. This is your destiny and you have me. Gods Kara, you have me."

Kara kissed him passionately as she undressed him so slowly and gently, she could feel him begin to completely relax into the situation. When he was naked, she began kissing him every-where and then said before taking the tip of his ridged penis into her mouth, "See we weren't going against the gods by me doing this yesterday." *Although it was great that you thought so when I was doing it,* she thought as she began lightly flicking her tongue across his frenulum, up and down, to get him more aroused and to stop thinking about everything so seriously.

Before she took him into her mouth she moved down to his balls and began gently licking them and caressing them lightly with her fingers. She was on her knees and looked up at him. They held eye contact for half a minute before she spoke, "Just tell me if you don't like it," she said playfully.

He wanted to tell her, 'To be serious,' but the words would not come out as she was already giving him so much pleasure and the idea that she was going to do this again made him more aroused than he had been in a long time.

Kara looked back down and began kissing the inside of his thighs, licking his penis up and down slowly, purposely avoid-ing the tip and then finally after countless minutes of teasing him began taking him into her mouth and sucking. Then she would lightly blow on it and she heard him gasp, 'Gods' and she smiled.

He was way too big to even consider deep throating him, she hated that anyway, so she just concentrated on what she was good at, keeping it nice, slow and pleasurable. She had never had any complaints before even though she had to admit to herself, she would not include fellacito as one of her top sexual skills. She looked up at him again and made eye contact just be-fore he was going to come and asked, "Do you want me to swallow your come or do you want it somewhere else?"

He couldn't think, *What a strange question*. "Swallow it."

She smiled and then continued, she had to bring him back, but she was smiling to herself thinking about the expression on his face when she asked. *Obviously pearl necklaces were not something that Alliance men did,* she thought. He came, and she swallowed it all and then wondered again at the taste of it, being just like human men, *Are we the Lost People?*

Tir looked down at Kara and pulled her up to him and embraced her. Then he began removing her clothing and said, "Let's sleep for a while now." And pulled her into bed with him as he held her close. Tir's curiosity got the better of him though and he had to ask, "Kara?"

"Hmm," she was almost asleep.

"Where do human men come if not in a woman's mouth?"

She opened her eyes and smiled thinking, *You are going to think this is another dirty human thing, I can feel it already*. "You could have come on my body somewhere or I could have spit it out."

"On the floor?" he asked disbelievingly. She could sense the next word, "Barbaric."

"Why?"

"It has to do with both the gods and hygiene, there is a myth about..." before he could continue, she stopped him.

"I am too tired to hear about it now. I want to sleep."

Kara fell asleep in minutes. When she woke the next morning, she vaguely remembered them having very slow sensual sex which he instigated during the night. She was relieved that she had been able to convince him that sex during pregnancy was fine. She wondered what other Alliance couples did. *Did they not have sex and just fellacito for nine months?* But then she thought about the amount of times he had already made her come and reasoned that maybe this was just the Alliance tradeoff between husband and wife as strange as it seemed. She was happy that had been able to dispel that quickly. The only thing that kept her sane she thought was his touch.

A few days later, Kara was talking to the bathroom mirror, practicing her Alliance pronunciation when there was a chime at the door. Mux came in with a lot of clothing and things in his arms. He laid them on the bed and then began hanging the clothes up in the wardrobe. She looked at the clothing and noticed that it was made from a much finer material than the one she was wearing and asked, "Are those for special occasions?"

"Some are, but most are for every day. Admiral Tir wanted you to have clothing that suited your rank now, especially since you are reluctant to even wear the one necklace, he gave you."

"How will I know which is which?" she asked looking at the dresses that all just looked very nice to her, boxy in that terrible Alliance cut, but made of beautiful material.

"I will show you. Also, in those boxes on the table is jewelry for you. It is important that you become accustomed to wearing it."

"Is this jewelry that the Admiral bought for me specifically or are these pieces he might have already had for a potential future wife?" Kara had found that Mux was a good source of cultural information.

"Both. A man begins collecting jewelry for a future wife when he becomes of marrying age."

"What is the marrying age?"

"Thirty-years old. Before that, a man is unable to marry."

Kara looked down at the jewelry, there was a lot of it and reflected, *He has been buying this for a future wife for the last 15 years, for someone he didn't even know.* "I find this so strange." She began opening the boxes and seeing the most gorgeous necklaces and bracelets she had ever seen. "I couldn't imagine wearing any of this."

"Aren't you happy with the jewelry?"

"It is all stunning. It's not that, it is your culture, it is so different," Kara explained. "I am sure an Alliance woman would have been very happy to receive this, or?" she questioned.

"Yes," he answered her patiently. As he saw Kara at all times of the day, he had more sympathy than most for her situation. He knew she was trying to understand their culture, but he reckoned it was just too much at once, they were at war and it was a very unusual circumstance, her being both Admiral Tir's prisoner and wife. "Men are publically, avid collectors of jewelry so that potential wives know what they will receive when they marry. Admiral Tir is said to have good-taste and values quality over quantity."

Kara looked at Mux stunned as she often did when he said these surprising things about their culture and tried to keep her mouth closed. It all seemed like something from medieval Earth. She closed the box to the necklace she was looking at and decided to change the subject. "Mux, Admiral Tir said he also ordered some human food. Could you bring some coffee to me and a list of what he bought?"

"Everything is the same as what you took from your ship before, coffee, tea, honey, salt, except the human owner, who was very curious about a human aboard an Alliance starship apparently, also included two other items and a personal message for you." He pulled a communicator out of his pocket and brought up the message and showed it to her.

> *Hello fellow human, I hope that you will be happy with your shipment. I am also including some chocolate and a bottle of wine in our appreciation and hope you will be a regular customer. Bon Appétit. Frank, Owner of the Earth Store, Alliance Empire*

"Where is the chocolate and wine?" Kara asked excitedly.

"I took it to the kitchen to keep with your other things," he replied casually.

"Bring all the chocolate and wine here, now." She had not had human chocolate or wine in a year. She was going to have it now. She knew she could still have a glass of wine while being pregnant and she needed to do it before Tir found out and had a heart attack and took it away from her. He had already removed the Alliance wine from his quarters. Even though John had told Tir it was fine he said, 'We are taking no chances Kara,' she was so tired of hearing that phrase from him.

Mux set out an exquisite black dress for Kara on the bed and took some of the jewelry from the boxes and put it next to the dress. "Put on this dress and jewelry with no fuss and I will bring you some of the chocolate and wine as a special favor, even though it is not meal time. I can imagine how you miss things from Earth." Mux, like many of the men onboard, were sympathetic to Kara's situation. They admired her and wanted to make her as comfortable as possible given the unusual circumstance. They were also all waiting in anticipation as well to see if human women could serve as replacements for the missing Alliance women from their own population, so they looked at Kara as if she represented the future of the Empire.

Kara took off her dress and put on this other one without even asking him to leave. Alliance citizens she had noticed cared little for being naked in front of one another, so she decided not to waste time between her and the chocolate by asking him to leave the room just for her modesty.

She then picked up the necklaces and Mux came to help her. "You know, we put these on and take them off in an order, shortest to longest and then longest to shortest," then he began putting them on her." After he finished putting on her jewelry, he decided that she looked like a proper Alliance woman now. "This suits you," he said taking away the other dress.

Kara thought as he put on the heavy necklaces, *I doubt this is what you signed up for when you joined the interstellar Alliance, poor boy.* "Now go and get the chocolate," she commanded him. Mux nodded and left. He was back in five minutes with the chocolate and wine. He set them down on the table in the dining room and she said with delight, "Swiss chocolate and French wine. Open the wine Mux."

He looked at the bottle and shook his head, "With what Captain Kara? I have never seen such an old-fashioned device. I don't know how to open this," he pointed at the cork.

"The Earth Store didn't send a corkscrew?"

"There were no devices in the shipment."

"Your sword. You can open it with your sword."

"Excuse me?"

"It might work."

"No. Show me what this corkscrew looks like and I will replicate one and never ask me to use my sword to open wine again."

"It goes against the gods?" she asked as everything fun in the Alliance seemed to be against the gods.

"No, a man who would use his sword for foolish tasks is not a real warrior."

"Oh," she said to the young man and tried not to smile. She wondered then if she should wait and see if Tir would use his sword. Then she went to the computer and tried to bring up a picture of a corkscrew, but as usual she was locked out of everything but the children's learning and the ship's internal communications.

Without thinking Mux accessed the guest user, "Show me now," he instructed Kara. Mux did not think that Kara would be able to read Alliance well enough to bring up the guest user herself.

Kara typed in 'human corkscrew for wine' and it came up.

Mux closed the guest access and the went to make one.

Kara could not help but smile, she quickly opened the guest user again and found external messages, she sent an encrypted message to any of the nearest human ship, which she knew was the *Silverado* because she had been helping Tir with their strategy for the next battle. Then she closed the user and went into the dining room.

It was not long before Mux returned, and she was enjoying a bottle of Bandol with dark chocolate thinking about escape. *The gods are telling me to get off the ship and back to Earth, if anyone is asking about these omens*, she thought as she ate the chocolate and drank the wine. After she had one glass of wine and had eaten half of the generous chocolate box, she left it all on the table, and said sternly to Mux, "Do not take that chocolate away. It stays there until I have eaten it all."

"But Captain," Mux protested.

"I will take the blame with the gods," she said as respectfully as she could. "And I don't think the ship is going to go down for this one misdemeanor of bad luck, do you?"

He didn't answer her, but they got back to their work of putting away these new things Tir had ordered.

"Can you explain these to me?" She held up some almost transparent stockings with designs that seemed to move on them with the light. Mux just looked at her dumbfounded and then she realized that he was definitely not the person to be asking because judging by his face expression these stockings were no doubt were supposed to be sexy. "Never mind. What is this?" she asked holding up a box with two bracelets in them.

"Marriage bracelets."

"So, these are what they look like," she said more to herself than Mux. They were two black and silver bracelets with markings on them. Some she understood and others she didn't. She asked Mux, "What does this mean?" pointing to a hieroglyphic.

"It is the Admiral's family name, now your family name."

"Great, I always wanted to be tagged like a dog," Kara said, and Mux gave her a disapproving look.

Kara opened another big box and it had a large pen in it, "What is this?"

Mux closed the lid of the box and moved it away from her, "The Admiral will explain it to you later."

"Tell me or I will tell him you let me have wine."

Mux looked at her as if she had betrayed him, "This is for binding tattoos. Some married couples get them."

"Binding, meaning you can never be with anyone else ever?"

"Yes, you will desire no other."

"How barbaric can the Alliance be?" she asked rhetorically.

Mux ignored her and then reminded her, "Captain Kara, it is time you go to the shrine and thank the gods. You can also pray to the goddess of house and home that the Admiral does not want you to take the barbaric binding tattoos. And just so you know, those tattoos are considered to be a very romantic gesture in the Alliance."

Kara just looked at Mux in disbelief. She did not understand this culture at all. *How could physically binding yourself to someone be romantic?* But then she reminded herself, *Isn't that what this whole marriage thing is about?*

Kara wanted to go through more of the things that Tir had ordered for her with Mux and ask him more questions about his culture, but she knew she had to go to the shrine. She reluctantly left him to put everything away. She walked out and immediately his guards were her shadows as they always were as she made her way to the shrine. It was always busy at this time of day and she had no doubt that was why Tir asked her to continually come at this time. She always walked directly to the fertility goddess's statue, said the short prayer, waited a minute or two, depending on her mood and then left.

As she was slowly making her way back to Tir's quarters, she feigned to be tired and asked to go to sickbay. Her guards of course took her directly there. She wanted to see John but unfortunately of course it was Doctor Siu coming forward to see her as she entered.

She tried to keep her mind as focused as possible on feeling ill, which wasn't very difficult as all she had to do was think about the hybrid growing inside of her.

"Captain Kara, please sit down. You must calm yourself."

Damn, she thought, *he is reading my mind.*

"This is not going to be a monster," he tried to comfort her. "It will be a beautiful child to start a new and peaceful chapter in both human and Alliance's lives."

"I don't think I can do it. I want to speak with John, I don't know anything about pregnancy, and I don't have access to a computer. I am scared," she was only have lying about being scared about being pregnant.

Siu nodded and brought John over. Siu did not leave them alone though.

"Are you feeling dizzy again?" John asked for something legitimate to say.

"Yes, it was my daily walk to the shrine. I always go an hour before the midday meal, but today I felt like I was going to pass out on the way back." What she was really saying was, 'I am going to try to escape when I go to the shrine.'

"Maybe you should change the time and you won't feel so light headed?"

Kara was pleased that they were easily talking with a hidden message about when to try and escape, "Tir asked me to go at that time, so I will continue to do so, I just wondered if this was normal?"

John put his hand on Kara's arm, "Yes, your body will be changing a lot. Don't stress." John was trying to say, 'Yes, I understand.'

Kara smiled and said she felt a bit better got up and walked back to Tir's quarters before she missed lunch. As she walked into Tir's quarters, Mux had just laid out her lunch. She sat down and ate with him watching her as no one was allowed to eat alone. Apparently, it did not matter if only one person was eating, and Kara wondered if this meant that Mux missed lunch every day, she couldn't meet John and she expected he did. "Why don't you ever eat with me?"

"I am here to take care of you, I am not your equal."

Kara sighed, she knew that was the answer before she asked and realized she did subconsciously to be reminded that these people were not her own and never would be. That she needed to focus on escape and not try to make excuses for them or justify staying.

Kara finished eating and then Mux left. When she was sure he was gone she logged into the guest account again on Tir's computer and saw a message for her. It was from Captain Jackson of the *Silverado*. He wrote,

> *Captain, I never knew you were also a fan of the wild west.*
> *The next time we are in Tombstone we should meet at the OK*

Corral. HJ

Kara looked at his message and tried to remember what happened at the OK Corral. She could not remember and if she searched for it, and someone noticed she would not be able to escape.

She closed the guest services and sat on the sofa trying to remember everything she could about the wild west. "Come on Rainer, your father loved that stuff. Remember," she whispered to herself. "Nothing is ever lost in the mind, it only takes longer to retrieve it," she said trying to inspire herself to remember.

She lay on the sofa then, her eyes closed going through everything she knew about that time-period in human history. Then she remembered a name and said out loud, "Wyatt Earp was in Tombstone." Then she thought to herself, *But what did he do? Was there a rescue at the OK Corral? What can I respond back?*

She lay on the sofa for 30 more minutes concentrating and then she jumped up, opened the guest computer and replied,

> *I hear that fight is something to see and takes place every two days at the same time, at about noon, but one should dress appropriately if entering from the actors' entrance.*

She sent it and hoped it made sense. The last battle would take place in two days and if she were able to get away from her guards, she would be able to escape. She knew the *Silverado* had cloaking technology and the one thing that humans did better than any other species in the galaxy was stealth. The *Silverado* could get in and out during the battle. Humans had technology to get through force fields quickly, disruptions that would go unnoticed in a battle.

Kara quickly checked her messages one more time before Tir returned and she was not disappointed.

> *It's funny you should say that. I have two friends that are actors in that reenactment. They say that they never use the actors' entrance but always the spectators and are there are*

noon sharp, but it's always confusing then with the spectators not quite realizing what is going on until the man who plays Doc Holiday says, 'I'm your huckleberry,' as late as 3PM.

Kara thought to herself, *Really Captain? I don't love the old west and I hope that you mean you are coming through the main docking bay at noon during the battle which will hopefully have begun by then.* Just then Tir walked through the door and she quickly closed the program. She could see on his face that he was trying to decide if he had just seen anything suspicious, so she took him off guard by saying to him in Alliance, "Welcome home husband."

Tir was dumbstruck when Kara spoke to him in Alliance. He knew that is what she had used as she had an accent suddenly and this was a set phrase that only existed in his language as one word. He recovered himself after a minute and then said the appropriate response, "I am home," which was a set response which was also only one word.

Kara's heart was beating so quickly, *Had he seen the message? Did I distract him enough to forget? Was he going to take away everything from me and keep her in the brig now?* She was watching him, waiting for a reply.

Tir knew he shouldn't be that surprised that she learned to speak Alliance as well as read. Humans were known to waste their time doing things like this. He knew that she would never gain the kind of fluency she needed to steal a ship, even though, without a doubt that was her intention. "You know you have an accent?"

She turned her translator off now so she would not be distracted by the English in her ear when she was trying to speak Alliance. "I know, but you can understand?"

He smiled at her, her accent was adorable. He had never heard an alien speak Alliance and now he wanted her to say lots of things. "I can understand you. Your accent is pleasing to listen to. What else can you say?"

"What do you want hear? Maybe you can teach me how you

would unlock an Alliance ship," she smiled.

"You know you will never be good enough to fool the computer. If I gave you your own ship, we would have to reset everything for you. Our security technology outstrips most of the galaxy."

"Tell me about it."

"Not a chance. But tell me, how have you learned to speak? I am impressed."

"The hieroglyphics program and the mirror in the bathroom," she did not want to involve Sera in this. "Humans can turn their translators on and off at will."

"Yes, the galaxy looks at you all and laughs about it. But I am not laughing now, I find this endearing even though I know you had ulterior motives."

She did not want him thinking about how far her ulterior motives would go today so distracted him again, "As you can see," she stood up so he could see the dress and her jewelry properly, "I am suitably dressed now according to Mux."

"And to me," he took in her full appearance, she was dressed still modestly, but as his equal. "I hope you like the jewelry?" He had never imagined that he would see a human wearing that jewelry when he bought it years before, but now it seems so natural.

"I have never seen anything these pieces of jewelry. It is all exquisitely made. I imagine an Alliance woman would have been able to appreciate much more than I can." She was fishing because she wanted to know if she had bought anything for her specifically.

Tir went into the bedroom then and looked through all the boxes. He returned to the sitting area with a couple boxes. He sat down across from her and handed her a small black box, "This I bought for you specifically. It is not small because I think so much less of you now, quite the contrary."

Kara gently took the box from his hand and opened it up. Inside was a small but beautiful barrette.

"I know you don't want to wear a lot of jewelry especially

when you are alone so much, so I thought, maybe you could wear this in your short hair," he finished and thought, *Gods, I am so inarticulate. She must think I am complete amateur when it comes to our relationship.*

Kara had never been given a piece of jewelry in her life. She was touched by his thoughtfulness and realization that what she wanted was not anything he had bought before knowing her. She looked up at him, "Thank you Tir. It is lovely." She took it out of the box, and he reached over and took it out of her hands and surprisingly put it in her hair. She was always amazed by his actions like this. She couldn't' help then to be reminded of the first time they were alone in his quarters and he combed her hair. Alliance men, or at least Tir, seemed to have a thing for treating her like a doll and she never knew what to do when he did these things.

He opened the second box he had brought out then and she knew these were the marriage bracelets. He took them out and held them in his hands so that she could see them. "Can you read these inscriptions?"

"Yes."

"So, you know what these are?"

"Yes."

"Good. We should put them on now. We will have to repeat the promises to each other again."

Kara didn't know why she was nervous all of the sudden, she was already married and pregnant.

He took her left wrist and put the bracelet on her and then he put his own on and said, "Kara of Earth," he left off her surname as they were technically already married, "I pledge my life to you."

She responded, "Tir Zu," she knew he was surprised she knew his surname, "I pledge my life to you." Kara jumped when the bracelets tightened automatically then, and she felt a pin prick in her left wrist. "What was that?"

"Just an initial activation to make them ours," he turned her wrist and showed her where it said children, "there will be a number there after we have a child and it will continue to grow, I hope."

She looked at him in disbelief, "And you all wear these things openly with your names and how many children and how long you have been married?"

"Yes, it is an honor to be married."

She looked down at the bracelet now and wished her dress covered her wrists but now understood why it did not. She felt sick again and went into the bathroom but didn't throw up, she just hovered over the toilet wishing she could throw up. Then she got up and splashed some ice-cold water on her face. When she emerged, she said, "Frank from the Earth store sent a bottle of wine and chocolate. I need to eat and drink this now. We have so much to celebrate," she said the last sentence sarcastically.

Tir followed her into the dining room and took the wine. "Not this."

"How do you not know this is just as dangerous?" she asked holding up the chocolate.

"Very little happens on this ship without my knowledge especially anything about you." He set the wine on a side table and poured them both some water and sat down. "This is a strange situation for us both, but Kara, this is destiny. We are meant to be together. The gods have blessed us. You will see."

"I am so tired of you saying that. I am here against my will and now seriously married."

"You were seriously married months ago too."

"I guess being tagged like a dog with all of my personal information on my wrist makes it real."

"You mean you can't lie to yourself about it?"

"Yes," she confessed.

He brought back the wine and poured her half a cup. "Relax. You are no one's pet." Tir looked at Kara and remembered Siu's advice not to put extra stress on her so he decided not to bring up the binding tattoos now.

"With all you Alliance men running around after me, I feel like it. I am used to taking care of myself, you won't even allow me to walk to the shrine and back alone."

"It is for your protection."

"At least let me eat with John tomorrow. I hate Mux watching me eat knowing he misses his lunch because of me."

"You can have the midday meal with John tomorrow," Tir said against his better judgement. But he rationalized it with himself, she was pregnant now, she would not want to leave. He didn't realize that humans saw fetuses as non-beings until they could survive by themselves and that escape was still very much on her mind.

The next day after visiting the shrine Kara met John in the mess hall for the midday meal. Although the guards shadowed, the mess was louder with so many voices they could not fully concentrate on her conversation with John.

"I was invited to the OK Corral," she said out of the blue, "by the captain of the *Silverado*."

"It is unfortunate you can't go," John said after a couple seconds trying to figure out what she was talking about or if she had completely lost her mind. "Remind me again, what time does that start? At night?"

"Before lunch tomorrow. The same time I usually go to the shrine to thank the gods for the child."

"Ah," he said as if this was the most boring thing in the world. "I expect I will be very busy in sickbay then, we are going into battle, probably in the morning. Siu has said to expect the worst as the Jahay will see this as a last-ditch effort."

"Yes," she agreed and then they held each other's eyes. She knew he would not be able to join her. He was not followed by guards, but he would also be killed on sight if he was caught trying to escape. She, as the Admiral's wife, would always have to be taken alive, or so she assumed.

"I am sure you are learning a lot that will help humanity when you return."

"Yes," he agreed and then said, "You should think twice about going to the shrine so much now that you are married and with child, Captain."

She dismissed his warning with a stern look and then they said their goodbyes which would hopefully be a goodbye for quite some time.

That night Tir did not come back to his quarters until very late. "Is everything alright?"

"Yes, just last-minute changes for tomorrow."

Tir got into bed pulled her close to him and then reached his hands down and pulled off her stockings without saying anything.

She became immediately aroused by his hands on her legs and cuddled closer to him.

He then put his hand on her hip though to keep her at an acceptable distance, "I just need to sleep now." Tir was asleep in minutes.

Kara's mind was racing from his words, *What if the plans have changed so much the* Silverado *can't rescue me?* She told herself that no matter what happened she needed to get to the docking bay by noon and she willed herself to sleep and she had a small thought she tried to stamp out, but couldn't that said, *And revel in these last moments next to him in the silence, because you will miss this.*

The next day the battle was vicious. The *Refa* was hit a couple times and the ship rocked with the impacts. Everyone was at their stations and she was left with one guard. She still went to the shrine as she always did. She only wore her barrette and marriage bracelet though as she did not want to be incumbered by all the other jewelry. She also wore three pairs of stockings under her dress, she was not leaving without those. When she walked out of the shrine the *Refa* was hit again and this time the lights went out momentarily, Kara did not wait, she ran as fast as she could away from her guard. There was so much confusion that she had lost him in no time, then she began running towards the docking bay. It was so obvious that this is where she would go, she knew the guard would sound the alarm and this would be the first place they looked, but it was also the place that she was supposed to be rescued from. She was running through corridors, trying to remember the way, but just as she saw the main doors, she was hit over the head by someone from behind her and crumpled to the floor with feet all around her.

Kara awoke in complete darkness. Her head hurt. She touched her head and winced, she could feel dried blood there. She tried to feel where she was, but she just felt cold metal. *Great,* she thought, *I am in a transport storage unit.* She wondered if she should scream for help or if it was better to remain quiet and see if she could somehow figure out a way out of the box, in complete darkness without a weapon or tool. She decided to try the latter first. Her fingers traced every inch of the box and she could not find anything that felt like a latch. She sat back and thought, *You were right Tir. The ship is not safe and now I have been abducted by your enemies instead of my people.* Suddenly Kara felt very tired again and decided to just sleep. Soon she would either die or be let out of the container she reasoned.

When she woke up next, she was in a bed and when she sat up and looked around the room, she was surrounded by all the sights and sounds of everything human. It was all so overwhelming. She almost began to cry.

She immediately got out of bed, felt dizzy, but it was only a minute until she steadied herself and then walked out the door to her room. She smiled that it just opened. It was unlocked, she was with her people and no longer a prisoner. She walked out into the ship's hallway looking for someone, but it must have been in the middle of the night as there was no one there and the hallways were only dimly lit. She decided to go back into her room then and ask the computer. One thing that was certain though, she had been rescued by her own people and she was no longer a prisoner. Relief washed over her.

In her room, she brought up the ship's general computer on the desk and found out that she was indeed aboard the *Silverado* and the mission was classified. She apparently was not even cleared to see it, so she had no idea if she was the only one who had been rescued or if they were heading back to Earth or what. She got back into bed then and thought about everything that had happened in the last weeks and made her plans now that she was free. The next thing she was going to do was try to get her female crew home before any of them become pregnant.

She quietly apologized to the unborn baby inside of her, "I am so sorry," her voice was barely a whisper, "I hope that if there is an afterlife like your father believes in, you will find it in your heart to forgive me for what I must do. I must protect humanity at all costs, even yours little one."

The next morning Captain Jackson was at her door with his doctor. She sat up. She thought, *The fates are cruel*. The *Silverado's* doctor was her former lover, Micah. They had been madly in love until she had abruptly ended it because she didn't want to have to think about him during the war. Kara ran her fingers through her short hair and then looked down and realized she was still wearing Alliance clothing, and nothing was more repellant to human men than Alliance dresses.

"Captain Jackson, thank you for retrieving me," Kara said and then to the doctor, "Micah, you don't know how good it is to see a familiar face."

"We could not let those zombies take one of our best, Captain," 'zombies' was a derogatory term humans used to refer to Alliance citizens because of their grey skin. "I am just happy to see that you are mostly unharmed. We ran some tests on you when you came onboard, the doctor is willing to abort that hybrid now. Micah insisted we wait for your consent, but I tried to tell him you would want it out of you as soon as possible." Captain Jackson was happy that he was not female as he could not imagine anything worse than having an alien growing inside of him.

"We can do it right now," said Micah. He put a hand on her shoulder sympathetically, "I am sorry for what they have put you through Kara. It must have been terrible." Micah imagined her being tied down and raped or restrained in a medical bed and artificially inseminated at best.

"I am sorry we had to knock you unconscious, we had to make it look like pirates, so that it did not look like a human operation," Captain Jackson explained. "It is so strange that they took you all prisoner to begin with. Your crew told us some crazy story about wanting human women, but we couldn't believe it until now," he trailed off with a disgusted look on his face.

Kara nodded understanding and then wanted to explain, "The Alliance has a demographics problem. They are at least at a 7% decrease in the female population and they want to use human women to fill in the gaps."

"What the ..." Captain Jackson said, his blue eyes reflecting his anger. "So, they want to create half Alliance half humans because their fertility is failing? Over my dead body. Doctor abort this abomination. There will be no hybrid zombie kids in the galaxy just because the Alliance has a problem."

"They believe we are some Lost People from their ancient mythology. They believe humans and Alliance are the same species."

"Religious fanatics. I am sure they are suffering from too much inbreeding or something," said Captain Jackson with disdain. "The war is over as of this morning. Yesterday was the final battle. Admiral Tir and his crew were too busy to notice your abduction until it was too late. It is a good thing that no one in the galaxy has figured out yet that we have cloaking technology. Just one more human trick, it is so convenient the rest of the galaxy thinking we know nothing and have nothing."

"I just wish we had cloaking technology on all of our ships," said Kara, "including mine. Where is the *Dakota*?"

"Waiting for you in orbit around Earth."

"Are we on our way there now?"

"Yes. Once you are on Earth, I doubt they will pursue you further, but now we need to be concerned about them abducting women. If it is not one thing it is another."

Kara had no idea how long Tir would pursue her or what he would do now, "I had so much information that would have helped the Jahay in the war, what a waste."

"It was doomed from the beginning, Captain. Thankfully, the Jahay are no longer a threat on our doorstep anymore and I guess we can thank the Alliance for that at least. It is a pity we won't' slip back into obscurity now if they pursue this Lost People nonsense. It will be good to say the baby died as soon as we reach Earth, maybe then they will think it is too difficult to hold on to human women and too difficult to combine the species."

"I will message the Admiral that the baby died as soon as we reach Earth to stop the search for me, maybe then the Alliance will pursue another avenue for their demographics issue, and we can work on getting my female crew off their capital planet."

"We will have to leave your female crew to the diplomats. There is no way we could get them off the Alliance capital planet. No doubt some deal can be struck when they come for the war reparations."

"Is it his, Admiral Tir's child?" Micah was horrified, "Kara, I promise you, if I ever get the chance, I will murder him for raping you," he said fervently.

Kara wanted to tell them that it was far from rape, but she couldn't. She knew if she admitted that then she would be subjecting herself to suspicion of being a spy, so she said nothing, and she felt guilty about that because she knew Tir was one of the last men in the galaxy who would ever rape a woman. *I am sorry Tir, but I must do this, or risk being accused of being a spy by my own people. They would never understand. Humans are just as racist as Alliance*, she thought hoping in a futile way, her thoughts would somehow reach him.

Micah looked at Kara, "Everything looks fine, I will prep sickbay and come and get you when I am ready. In the meantime, you should try and take it easy now. I will have some other clothing brought to you, so you can burn that," he said looking at her Alliance dress with revulsion.

She thanked them both and then the captain left her with an invitation to dinner for tomorrow evening. She of course accepted. She needed to find out everything that had happened in the months that she had been away.

The doctor lingered, "Kara, is there anything else you need?"

Kara looked at Micah, they had been passionate lovers the year before. She could not deny that she still found him very attractive, he was tall and muscular with brown skin and light brown eyes.

Micah looked at Kara and his heart was beating fast, he was still, very much in love with her. He wanted to take her in his arms now and tell her that it would all be okay. She was looking at him now in a way familiar to him. So, he took a chance and he sat next to her on the bed and put his hand on her cheek lightly, "What a mess," he said softly, "but we have you now," and then he slowly kissed her. Chastely at first but then soon his tongue was testing her lips, her mouth and it felt so right for him, to have his Kara back.

Am I really kissing Micah now? she mentally questioned her morals and sanity. His mouth felt so warm compared to Tir's and the stubble on his face rubbing against her skin a little roughly, made her question what she used to found attractive now somewhat repulsive, *Have I forgotten what it is like to be with a human man so quickly?* She found his touch soothing but not right sexually. She gently pulled back but was still touching his chest. "Micah, it is so good to see you, I cannot even express it properly, but I have been through a lot. I don't think I can do this now."

"Let me comfort you Kara. Let me bring you back to humanity," he began kissing her again and she acquiesced for a time until she pulled back again.

Kara could see the desire in his light brown eyes and for a couple of seconds she thought that maybe she should do this to separate herself in a completely physical and intimate action away from Tir. That by sleeping with Micah, it would end her confusion. But then, she brought herself back to reality. "I can't do this. I am pregnant with another man's baby. I feel terrible." *And I married him,* she thought, but she definitely was not going to mention that barbaric act, but she could not help but look down at the bracelet.

"Not another man, a zombie, an Alliance and he raped you. You owe him nothing." Micah felt sorry for her and just held her close to him. He noticed that she smelled differently and concluded it must be the different soap she had to use or food that she had had to eat with the Alliance.

"I still feel…" she trailed off, she did not know what she felt, except that to sleep with him would be wrong, even though her body thought it was a good idea. She realized that she really did have feelings for Tir and that as much as she wanted to escape and be free, she would still miss him and his touch. She didn't want to be married of course, but she wished that things could have been different, and they could just be together, but that would never be. She was going to go back to her old life and if anyone ever tried to take her again, she would die fighting.

"I understand. We can take care of the pregnancy. I understand that none of this is easy. This child represents too much to the Alliance to let it live. Think of what would happen if those floodgates opened, we would not be able to protect ourselves."

"I can't explain this feeling. I feel like I am going to kill an innocent and I know I will regret this for the rest of my life, but I cannot keep it either. I just wish all of this had never happened."

"How could you regret killing a child begotten of rape from a monster…." Kara interrupted him.

"He is not a monster."

"Don't tell me you have feelings for him? Was it rape or not Kara?" Captain Jackson had questioned him about what kind of woman Kara was before they decided to help her. He was concerned that she was a spy for the Alliance.

"I don't know," she admitted quietly looking into his eyes hoping she would find some understanding there.

"Stockholm Syndrome," he said confidently diagnosing her and hoping that she was not a spy. "Stop thinking about him. He has convinced you to think that you liked him, maybe loved him, by the way you are talking. Kara, listen to me, we have rescued you. It will take some time, but you will recover and see your captors for what they truly are, barbaric criminals. They abducted you and raped you for their own greedy purposes. Give yourself time to readjust. I am going now and will return shortly. Relax, you have survived this. You are strong, and you are safe."

When Kara was alone, she opened the computer and accessed her messages, she had so many but there was one that stood out that was sent only five hours ago. She could read the sender's name in Alliance, 'Admiral Tir Zu', she opened it not knowing what to expect.

> *Kara, I know you were taken and are unable to return. I will come to Earth for you. Tir*

Kara looked at the message written in Alliance. She knew he had done that on purpose. Her tears began to silently fall and hit her hands as she hesitated to send a reply. If she replied, he would know where she was, but she decided he was not coming after her now anyway, so she wrote,

> *Tir, The baby died. Don't come for me. Kara*

BOUGHT

Tir read Kara's message and wondered two things, first if she had been forced to have an abortion and second, if she really never wanted him to find her. He got up from his desk and went to pray in front of his shrine. He moved the fertility goddess back and moved the god of war forward. He lit a small candle and prayed for forgiveness. He unsheathed his short sword and made a cut down the center of his left palm, letting the blood put out the candle flame.

He was angry. Angry with himself for not taking better care of Kara.

He had gone over their last day together in his mind over and over again. He should have addressed her concerns about their child being the catalyst to destroy humanity more seriously. Something that he thought was so preposterous, he had just dismissed. He had not taken her fears seriously enough to explain to her that that was not what the Alliance had in mind. They had been at war and he had not had the time or patience for her small human concerns. Now, he only had himself to blame for the death of the child. It did not matter if she chose to have the abortion, she was forced to do it or if she lost the child from the escape itself, he put the fault on himself for her not believing in their shared destiny.

Then he thought about their relationship. Physically they were well-matched, suitably sexually attracted to each other, but again, he blamed himself for not being as emotionally attentive as he should have been when she was onboard. He knew that she was struggling with everything that had happened to her, but he thought there would be time after the war to help her settle into her new position as his wife in the Alliance. For this misstep, he only had himself to blame for her running away. He knew humans' reputation well enough to know they would make it look like an abduction so that no one could be blamed, but that she had escaped. He had interrogated her doctor but he of course said he knew nothing about it. Tir didn't think it was worth threatening the man over it. He did not go and seemed genuinely interested in trading human medical knowledge for Alliance.

Tir looked at the small white statue of the god of war and said quietly, "I will go to Earth and bring her back. I will right this wrong. Do not give up on us. We will fulfill our destinies."

He stood up and went back to his computer. He rebuttoned the collar on his uniform which he had loosened after his shift and opened a video message to his mother who was a senior member on the High Council. His fleet was not far from the Alliance border, so they could talk in real time.

"Tir," she said pleased to see him on the screen. "You are not coming home, are you?"

"No, I have requested that I be the one to go to Earth and oversee the war reparations and at the same time retrieve my wife," this would normally be left to someone below him.

"Are you going to kill her for leaving you?" Tir's mother had been shocked when he had told her that he had married Kara. So much so that she had not replied to his message for days.

"No," he looked at his mother scandalized. "I am going to bring her back. She was abducted." They both knew she escaped but to run away from your spouse carried heavy consequences in the Alliance.

"Are you sure she was abducted and didn't intentionally run away?"

"Mother, have some sympathy."

"Tir, I do. But I think you are so blinded by your infatuation for this woman you can't see the situation clearly. The rumors of you two have even reached us here on the capital planet your fights and your love-making during a war. Everyone thinks that this wild human has driven you to it, no doubt that was your plan, to make human women look so sexually irresistible that every Alliance man would want to marry one. It was well-played until she ran away. I mean, was abducted."

He was not going to discuss his sexual life with his mother, "She did not run away. She was abducted during the last battle. I need the High Council's permission to offer the humans universal credits, weapons, and technology. I will be there in three days."

Tir's mother looked at him and sighed, "How much do you think they will ask for? Remember they did lose this war, you should not have to offer them much."

"You know this is about our future relationship with Earth too? We want humans to like us so that more women come to the Alliance freely. I don't want to make it a habit of targeting human ships just to take the women and send them to the Alliance. I will offer them minimal compensation, but for Earth, it will seem extravagant as they are so poor. I will also need access to our family accounts to secure the release of Kara. She has been arrested and being tried as a spy. There is no doubt that will be expensive."

"Humans are living up to their reputation in the galaxy as being untrustworthy and impulsive, aren't they? Are you sure you want her back? Maybe you should let her stay in prison, and you marry someone else."

"Mother, do I have access to the accounts or not?"

"Of course, you do. I just hate to see you having to buy your wife back."

"I must admit, I was not the best husband to her when she was onboard."

"You were at war, you had other things on your mind Tir. She should have honored her marital pledge to you."

"That is true, but I also made the mistake of assuming she

would be happy to be married to me, which was not the case. We like each other to be sure, but she is not religious. Humans believe in nothing these days, and I did not take the time to properly explain things to her. I thought our physical connection would be enough for her to eventually accept her destiny, but it wasn't. This is my fault and because of this, I will not bring her home directly. I plan to keep her with me and make amends for my past behavior."

"Why would she not be happy to be married to you? There is nothing wrong with you. And she is human. Why didn't she feel honored that you chose her?"

"I don't think she ever saw herself getting married or doing anything but dying in her ship during the war. It was quite a surprise to be thrown into a marriage, no matter how attractive she might have found me. And humans have been isolated for so long, they still see themselves as quite important in the galaxy, despite every fact telling them the opposite," he could not help but smile then, "In some ways, it is good they have some pride. It will make it easier for them to act like Alliance citizens once they accept that is what they are."

"It is a good thing that they are so good-looking or else they would already be punished for this pride. And did you tell her that you were the successor to the imperial throne? Maybe that is why she ran away, she was scared of being killed for it."

"I told her I was the successor to be Emperor and she was unimpressed and uninterested. I think she was more upset that she might have to do something rather than just be in her starship and not live on Earth. I know, it does not make any sense, but humans seem to be, as we have often noticed, focused on the wrong things at the wrong times."

"Gods Tir, I still can't believe you married a human. Anyway, we digress. It helps that she has been imprisoned by her own people. It doesn't make your behavior look quite so bad, but you should not keep her on ship, you should send her home to us to learn what is expected of an Alliance woman. Your sister Hes is so curious to meet her."

"No, I want her with me to make amends for the past months, then we will see what she wants. I doubt she would want to live on the capital planet even for a short amount of time." *And I am worried for how my sisters would treat her, an alien, a human.*

"If she becomes pregnant, she will have to come home to us. Your doctors cannot help a woman on a starship. It goes against the gods Tir. Whatever you are thinking about that, abandon that plan."

Tir did not want to go into that with his mother. He knew she would be very upset by the whole thing and then would not help him now with the High Council. "Of course," he said. "Now, about the High Council's approval?"

"I will push this through and arrange a new rendezvous with new Ambassador to Earth. We cannot have old Tui there anymore now that we actually need to do something other than just monitor the comings and goings of humans. We will all be praying for you. May the gods grant you success."

"Even if I am unworthy," he answered his mother with the response to the set phrase and then they both signed out.

A small ding at Kara's quarters onboard the *Silverado* announced an ensign's arrival. "Here are some clothes for you Captain. Do you want me to take that Alliance dress and throw it out an airlock?"

She forced a smile at the young ensign, "Thank you, no. I will take care of it myself." Kara took the human fleet uniform from the ensign and dismissed him.

She began taking off the Alliance dress and realized it was impossible to do without thinking of Tir. How he touched her so tenderly and she tried to dispel those memories from her mind but couldn't. In the end, she just let them play out as she undressed and tears were streaming down her cheeks silently. She smiled sadly as she took off two of the three pairs of Alliance stockings she had on and folded them with the dress. She left one pair on. She could not help but remember that his cool grey hands on been on these stockings less than a day before. She tried to think about something else then as she put on some underwear and a bra that was supposed to be her size but was too small now, then zipped up her human fleet uniform. Once she was dressed, she looked down at the folded black Alliance dress and decided she would keep it. She did not want to admit to herself why, so she just put it in the small closet and closed the door.

Kara looked at herself in the mirror and thought, *This is the first step, next step, stop crying.* She wiped her eyes. Then she noticed the barrette in her hair and she gingerly touched it. She looked at her reflection, her eyes were red from crying, "Take it out Rainer," she said quietly to herself and then with shaky hands she removed the barrette and put it in her pocket. She thought about putting it with the dress, but she wanted to keep it close. He had given that to her and for all the terrible things he had done, there was a small part of her that did really like him and an even larger part of her that could forgive him now that she was out of the situation and back with her own people. Finally, she tried to take off the marriage bracelet, but it would not budge even after several attempts and 20 minutes of trying. She decided that for the moment it didn't matter because there would be very few humans who knew what it was and as long as she wore long sleeves no one could see it anyway.

Another ding at her door and Micah was there, "Are you ready Kara?" He could see that she had been crying and he felt sympathy for her.

"Yes, let's go," she tried to speak without any emotion. She had mixed feelings about this abortion. She had never thought about abortion before. It had never occurred to her that she would have to consider it for herself, but here she was now and it was the moment of truth. Unprepared, but then she thought, *Is anyone ever prepared to think about abortion until they need to make the decision for themselves?* She tried to console herself that this was the right thing to do. It was a hybrid child, so easily conceived that it would only increase the chances of humanity being all-consumed by the much larger Alliance Empire. But without any way to stop it, she heard Tir's voice in her head saying, 'It goes against the gods, Kara.' She had no doubt that this absolutely would go against the gods if there were any. But she was not religious, and she quieted that voice in her head down by thinking, *This has nothing to do with my or Tir's religious beliefs, but everything to do with taking a life and whether or not I believe that this is a life and what this life would represent to the both our civilizations. The birth of a returned people, if indeed humans are the Lost People as the Alliance believes, or the beginning of a wave that could wipe out the uniqueness of humanity to fuel the Alliance's demographics issue.*

Micah spoke to her as they walked into sickbay, but she was not listening, all she kept thinking was, *Am I a murderer of an innocent or are these just cells? Am I saving humanity or just proving I am a savage as all the other species in the galaxy claim humans to be?* As they walked into a deserted sickbay and Micah led her to the back, she was overcome with angst and confusion. She followed Micah's instructions though and laid down on the medical bed after removing some of her clothes, but after a few minutes said, "No, stop. I can't do this Micah."

"Kara?" Micah asked as he put down his scanner.

"I know it sounds like I have lost my mind, but I can't do this now. It is still early enough that I can do this back on Earth, right? I am too confused to do this now."

Micah sighed, "Kara, I can't force you to do this now, but as your friend and your doctor, I recommend it and a good therapist. You have been through a lot." Micah was also disappointed not to be the first one to look at a human-Alliance hybrid and be able to write a paper on it.

Tears were in her eyes and she said softly, "Don't be ridiculous Micah we were never friends," and he gave her a sympathetic smile, "I need time. I will do it. I just can't right now, but I need you to record it as an abortion, so I don't look suspicious. I know I won't keep it."

He gave her a disapproving look, "I understand your concern, but I can't do that," this hybrid would not just be a normal abortion, it would be saved and studied. "I don't think you are a spy as it wouldn't make any sense. The Alliance have already proven that they can take what they want from us without asking, they wouldn't need convert any citizens to be spies. But I know that some people, like Captain Jackson think too highly of Earth and like to believe we are worth spying on. And there are those onboard who find it odd that you were so effortlessly rescued and that your doctor remained onboard *the Refa* as a prisoner."

"Please Micah, listen," tears were falling freely down her cheeks, "I have killed so many in this war, I just can't right now, but Captain Jackson will definitely think I am a spy if I don't, but I am not."

"This hybrid is an abomination Kara. You are so confused." He put a hand on her shoulder and said, "Trust me and do this now."

"Please Micah, give me more time but mark it as done, just between you and me for old time's sake. Will you do that for me?"

"The best I can do for you is to just note it that you came here for this procedure but nothing more. I would also ask that when you are ready, and I am sure once you come to your senses, you will be ready, you must do the abortion with me. As for everyone else, Captain Jackson will not ask but just assume that it is done. If anyone else asks, this falls under doctor patient confidentiality so I will not say one way or another, but that only goes so far. If you are arrested and put on trial, if I am asked, I will tell the truth. And if you wait too long, the truth will show itself soon anyway."

"I understand Micah, thank you. I owe you."

"You owe me nothing Kara. I always knew you had a conscious in there somewhere I am just surprised it is showing itself now for this hybrid child." Micah could not forget their last argument when they were still lovers. He had wanted to become more serious and have a child together and Kara had said to him,

'I would never want to be a mother to our child.' And now he looked at her and wondered, *Are you a spy Kara? Do you really want to live as a wife to this zombie? Do you think you love him?* And jealously and despair rose up inside of him as he watched her walk out of sickbay.

Kara spent the rest of the day in bed. The *Silverado's* counselor came to see her, but Kara sent her away. She said she would just like to be alone today. The counselor said that she would return tomorrow.

Kara laid in her bed and looked at the metal ceiling. She was happy to be back with her own people, but she questioned herself why she was not happier or more relieved. She fell asleep thinking about everything that had happened over the last few months and of course there was just one person she kept thinking about, Tir. She wondered if he was in pursuit of the *Silverado* now or if he would have given up and decided that maybe he was wrong, and they were not destined for each other after all. She had no idea how Alliance marriages worked. She wondered if they could be just as easily dissolved as they were created. She fell asleep thinking about all this.

She awoke in the early morning and felt sick. She got up and went to the toilet and was happy nothing in human bathrooms talked. She threw up. In between the acid taste of vomit, she saw and tasted a bit of the chocolate and thought about Tir again. Then she whispered to the vomit filled toilet, "Stockholm syndrome," and flushed it.

Once the queasiness had passed, she went to the *Silverado's* mess hall got herself a coffee and piece of bread. She did not like all the curious looks the *Silverado's* crew was giving her though and ended up taking her coffee and bread back to her temporary quarters. There, she sat down in front of the computer and began reading about everything of interest that had happened since she had been taken prisoner aboard the *Refa*. Nothing she read surprised her.

The human fleet had tried to stay back and out of the war

between the Jahay and the Alliance as much as possible, to keep human causalities low. Kara read it and thought, *And we are not even ashamed about this.*

No humans were elected to the Galaxy Court this year, not that a human had ever been elected into the Galaxy Court. Every year, a new Galaxy Court made up of 10,111 members was elected from all the civilizations of the galaxy. The only requirement was that a civilization must have a universal technology rating of at least three. Humans had a technology rating of barely four and because of that, other species did not think humans could be trusted to sit on a committee that tried to keep some unbiased record and order in the galaxy. Humans were always complaining that the galaxy was prejudice against them, but Kara had a different reflection after being aboard the *Refa* and living with the Alliance, she had to admit, the Alliance was more advanced in many more ways and maybe it was right, the galaxy's distrust of humans, it was not just human technology that was unevolved but their culture as well, there was very little structure or societal recourse for crimes, unlike many of other cultures in the galaxy. Kara, of course, preferred human culture to Alliance, but she had to admit, she could see where other civilizations might find faults with the way humans governed themselves and interacted with other species.

A new restaurant on Earth had opened and it encouraged diners to masturbate during the desert course with a vibrator specifically designed to accompany the dish and she thought, *And we wonder why no one takes us seriously?*

Then she was surprised to see as breaking news across the bottom of the news screen that Earth's government had already set a date to begin negotiating war reparations with the Alliance. *That is fast,* she thought, *Of course, they are. They want to keep all of those human women from the* Dakota *in the Alliance without causing too much attention to themselves. And probably retrieve me,* she also thought solemnly. She closed the computer then, she didn't want to think about it.

It wasn't long before the day passed. The councilor, as promised, had come to see her and they talked for hours about her capture, captivity and abortion. Kara did not say whether she had had the abortion or not, she just let the councilor believe that she had. She also didn't mention getting married because the councilor didn't think to ask it, as she was mainly focused on Kara's readjustment back into human society after having been kept as a sex slave. That is what the councilor had called her a 'sex slave'. The councilor had told her that the rapes had not been her fault even if she had not fought back. Kara did at this point try to say that it had not been rape any of the times, but the councilor had already made up her mind about what had happened. Kara felt incredibly guilty now that Tir was a documented rapist. The councilor asked her to sign off on their discussion and information received. Kara didn't want to do this.

"Do you mind if you change that, he didn't rape me," Kara said seriously, but gently.

"I understand that you are confused. This is called Stockholm syndrome. I have written that here too. It is because of this, you are trying to protect your captors. Please sign Captain Rainer," the councilor was forceful now and Kara knew that she was not going to backdown, but neither could she.

"I can't sign this. It was not rape."

"Captain, I understand that you believe that right now. I would not let you back on duty soon anyway. I am signing you up for regular sessions with someone on Earth to help. Just relax, none of this is your fault and given some time, this will all become clear to you."

Then the councilor left, and Kara felt even more confused. *Did Tir rape her?* she questioned herself. *No, it was definitely not rape. Forced marriage absolutely, but she wanted him every time as wrong as that was.*

That night Kara had dinner with Captain Jackson in his personal quarters. She was happy to have human food again, it was so good, she ate a lot and kept commenting to Captain Jackson how good it was. She had to listen to a lot of nonsense propaganda about how if humanity was just given a chance, the rest of the galaxy would give us the respect he thought we deserved. Kara did not believe any of that. She saw the facts as they were, and humans were undeniably almost last in everything because they were the last to this galactic technology party. She wished that people would just accept that and start from there, but then she reasoned sweet smelling lies were always better. She listened to the Captain politely, thanked him again for rescuing her and hoped that she would never have to have dinner with him again as he was just as racist against aliens as they were against humans.

On her way back to her temporary quarters she ran into Micah, who she suspected had been waiting to pass her in the hallway. "Kara, I want to talk to you."

"Is this about my health?" She really did not want to be alone with him right now. She had had some wine and was obviously emotionally vulnerable. He would only add to her confusion.

"Not officially. I am just worried about you, as a friend."

"I am fine, just ask the councilor."

"Yes, I read her notes. I don't think you should be alone right now." He began walking with her towards her quarters.

When they arrived at her door, they both stopped. She did not open the door.

He touched her cheek as if they were still lovers, "Kara, let me comfort you."

"Micah, we are no longer together."

"But Kara, part of your confusion is that you have been with aliens. Let me remind you..." his hand was on her arm gently stroking her.

Kara felt weak. She wanted to be held, but then she looked at him and thought, *But not by you.* "No Micah. I want to be alone. Good night. "

Micah accepted her answer and then wished her a good night all the while thinking, *There is something not right about all of this. We always have comforted one another even when we were not exclusively lovers.*

Kara went into her small quarters and sighed. She looked in the mirror and said out loud, "I don't know you anymore. Turning down Micah?" Sex with Micah had always been something that she sought for comfort. He was perfect in that way. Even before they had a serious relationship, they had always had a sporadic sexual relationship. Now she was turning him down when she could probably benefit from jumping back in with a human.

She took off her uniform and all her other clothing as well, everything but her Alliance stockings. She turned off the lights and got into the bed, closed her eyes and began thinking about Tir. Wishing that she could have him and her human life both. She ran her fingers over her sensitive breasts and then down to her inner thighs. Remembering how he always used to kiss her there. She started to feel her arousal increase at the thought of what was next. She brought her fingers up to stroke her vulva and pull a little on the hair there, just like he liked to do. She could hear his voice in her head saying, 'And I like this distinctly human hair,' as he would pull on it. Then she began rubbing her vulva lightly, long and wide strokes with her entire hand slowly, while she thought about him. The way his large strong hands would touch her. It was not long before she changed to using her fingers and rubbing her clitoris, lightly at first but then faster, with much more pleasure to quickly bring herself some release. She remembered how he had promised her to know her body as well as his to bring her to climax within minutes, just as she could do for herself, after a year of marriage. She smiled to herself and thought, *But you had almost managed to be able to do that after only a couple of months.* She wondered, *Will I ever be able to find another I am so physically compatible with? Is this why I miss him? I miss his physical touch only?* She drifted off to sleep with her hand still on the top of her thigh as Tir used to do.

The next morning, they reached Earth and Kara was relieved

when she walked into the very familiar Space Dock One. It was loud, noisy and utterly human. From there, she and Captain Jackson took a transport down to headquarters. Once there, they were ushered through some rooms and finally were confidentially talking about her experience during the war on the *Refa*. She did not mention the marriage and they didn't ask. Kara was told that she would need to speak to the Earth Ambassador to the Alliance about negotiating for her female crew and provide him with as much information as she could about the Alliance. He was on his way back from the Alliance and would arrive tomorrow. She was dismissed then, and she thought that the worst was over.

Kara went home. She stood outside her apartment building and the smart technology recognized her and opened the door, the same happened with the door to her apartment. After she walked in, she sat down on the sofa that she had made and cried for so many things, for being home again, for the loss of a baby that she knew she couldn't keep but couldn't find it in herself to get rid of either and for never being able to be with Tir again. She began to wonder if this is what love felt like, this complete aching for someone, or if this really was destiny. She wiped her tears and thought, *Destiny is so stupid.*

She got up then, went into her small yellow kitchen, opened the door to her balcony, even though it was autumn and a bit chilly, it did not feel cold anymore after her days on the Alliance ship, and watched the people go by below and tried to balance her emotions by the familiar rings of the trams going by and the sound of the people's footsteps. After several minutes she closed the door and poured herself a glass of wine. She drank it while she looked at her empty, colorful apartment and wondered if this would be her future forever, alone here.

After she finished the small glass of wine, she went into her bedroom, put on her pajamas and called her parents on a video call. They were very happy to see her. She did not tell them she had been abducted or any of that. She just said she had been away with the war. Her family operated strictly on a the-less-information-the-less-awkward for us all basis. They liked each other but were not close. Her parents were artists and she was in the military, there was very little middle ground. Her mother called her a murderess once and that was when she decided to keep them at an arm's length.

Kara then checked her messages, but there was nothing new there, so she pulled the blue velvet curtains on her ancient four-poster bed closed and went to sleep. As she drifted off, her mind wandered to the time she told Tir about her apartment and this bed and she could not deny that she missed him. She suddenly got up to retrieve the barrette from her pocket and held the cool piece of jewelry in her hand as she fell asleep.

Kara was dreaming about Tir. He was putting the barrette in her hair and she kissed him. She told him that she loved him for the first time, and this made him so happy. He picked he up and kissed her even more passionately, refusing to put her down for several minutes. When he finally did set her down, he took all of her clothes off except for the barrette. He was kissing and licking her whole body as he stood naked in front of him. Suddenly the doctor was there too watching, and Kara was even more aroused at that thought that they would both touch her. Tir whispered in her ear, "Do you want Siu to lick you too? He is so curious about humans."

"I want him to," she replied.

And then Kara had two Alliance men touching, kissing and licking her all over. She had never had four hands and two mouths on her at once before and she found the situation almost intoxicating. They carried her to the bed and continued to touch her. Sui was groping her breasts with his skilled hands and Tir was kissing around her inner thighs, occasionally making her jump with the sensations.

Then she was awaked by a noise outside and she opened her eyes and couldn't remember where she was. But it only took a couple of seconds for her to be comforted by the familiar sounds of the city around her. It was early morning. The tram bell. She smiled, *I am home.* She pushed back the velvet curtains and got out of bed, made herself a coffee and then checked her messages again. She almost dropped her coffee when she saw one from Earth's Ambassador to the Alliance.

> *Captain Kara, Please read the following article and meet me in my office as soon as you can this morning. Ambassador to the Alliance, Lora Lane*

Kara opened the attached article which brought her directly to the Galaxy Court's information page and an article about her recent marriage. Their military identification pictures had been used. She read the short article and swore out loud. The article made their marriage not only look romantic but almost like some kind of Cinderella story. She knew, of course, he had told her that he was an important person in his society, that he was successor to the Emperor, or that he had been. But it had all just seemed so alien, outside her comprehension. But now, looking at it in black and white, she understood why he had told her that if she escaped her own people would think she was a spy as preposterous as that was. But she had to admit, the galaxy must be looking at this article and saying to one another, 'This cannot be real, a human?' She hoped that people would question the Alliance's motives, but as she read though some of the comments on the gossip pages that were already discussing it, she realized that people weren't that clever. She was being accused of a lot of things, espionage, deceit, and witchcraft, which she particularly liked, "Better to be a witch than a spy," she said quietly out loud to herself.

She took a long hot shower and then put on her uniform and went to go speak to Earth's Ambassador to the Alliance, however, she was arrested as soon as she walked in the government building. She did not try to claim ignorance or her innocence to guards who knew nothing but that she should be arrested. It was not a long walk to the human fleet headquarters' jail, and she was put into a cell. There was no window, so she had no idea how much time passed before she had a visitor.

An older woman with silver hair, deep wrinkles and bright pink lipstick came in. She was wearing an old suit of the same hot pink as her lipstick. She looked at Kara and said, "I am your council. You are being tried as a spy, which is probably no surprise to you. If you do not want to go to court you can tell the man who has been impatiently waiting to see you all day in the hallway, I was late," she explained with a smile, "everything. I told him though, I don't think you are the type to give up any information and that he had been sent on a fool's errand. He didn't like that as you can imagine. So, what is it going to be Captain?" She hoped that Captain Rainer would chose to go with her rather than a backhanded deal with the military. She had heard the rumors that the Captain was still pregnant with the hybrid child and no doubt the would squeeze all the information out of her about the Alliance and take the child for scientific research as well.

Kara stood up and moved to stand in front of the older woman with just a transparent forcefield between them, "Councilor, I am not a spy."

"Sure, you are not. You sent all of your female crew to the Alliance capital planet, you stayed aboard Admiral Tir's ship for months and then just you were able to 'escape' at the end of the war. Now this morning we read that you are married to this zombie meant to be Emperor of the Alliance Empire. Tell me Captain, if you are not a spy then what are you?"

"This doesn't make any sense. If I were a spy why would I so openly be married?"

"Well, that is the thing isn't it? You were not open about it. In fact, you mentioned it to no one until now. Don't you think that is a bit suspicious? No doubt one of your enemies had that article published."

"I was embarrassed about being married that is why I did not mention it. I just wanted to put my whole Alliance experience behind me. I thought if I left and didn't mention it, the marriage would have just disappeared. I am not a spy. I was forced to marry an Alliance man. I was forced to send my crew away."

"Sure. Now do you want to go to court or do you want to tell all your Alliance secrets to the man from your fleet waiting behind me?"

"I am not a spy," Kara said defending herself.

The older woman sighed, "Look, between you and me I think it's better if you just tell them all you know and maybe then they will grant you clemency since obviously you are so naïve and were clearly forced into this. Maybe if this is really your lucky day, you can have your old life back."

"This is ridiculous. Why would the Alliance spy on us? We have nothing they want." But she as soon as she said it, she knew she was wrong. They wanted human women and any information about fertility.

"If they wanted nothing then why did you tell Captain Jackson that they wanted human women?" She looked at Kara sternly. "Now are you going to go with me and do this the hard way or go with the guy behind me?"

"Councilor, I want to go to court. I might be stupid being coerced into marriage and sending my female crew away, but I would never betray my people."

"Good," said the older woman. "I will register the documents and we will begin to go through the motions. You realize this is going to go very quickly as our government will want this done before the Alliance arrives."

"When do they arrive?"

"In three days, I suspect the next three days are going to seem very long for you. I have already put in the order for you to be monitored so that there will be no bad treatment of you, but you know how things are here. I will see you tomorrow."

Kara watched the woman go and as she opened the door, she heard her say, "I told you you were wasting your time. She's mine."

Kara sat down on the small cot and thought, *What would be the benefit of trying me as a spy?* and it was not long before she realized it was obviously for more leverage against the Alliance.

She wondered then if her own people would really abuse her while she was in this cell. *If the Alliance was really as strong and ruthless as they were rumored to be, wouldn't that defeat the purpose of keeping me here? They would have less leverage if I was beat up.* However, it did occur to her, that if they threaten her with physical violence, she probably would tell them more about the Alliance and then they would have even more leverage and her heart sunk. *Well, I might be still having that abortion from being beat up here,* she thought with a heavy heart. It also occurred to her that if Tir wanted her back he might negotiate harder if she had been injured. She could not help but be reminded of how he looked after her physically, almost as if she were a precious doll.

Tir's first officer slide a memo across to him on the open computer screen between them in the conference room. Kara had been arrested as a spy. Tir looked at it unemotionally and then said, "This was unfortunately expected. They are barbarians."

"Obviously, they think this will give them more bargaining power."

"And this is why no one likes dealing with humans." Tir had the Alliance 's new Ambassador to Earth brought in, "The humans have arrested my wife for espionage. I would like you to remind them that she is my wife and an Alliance citizen and that by the Galaxy Court ruling of 4587 no citizen of dual-citizenship can be tried for a crime without the approval of the other government."

"This is true Admiral, but we still have an ambassador there and I think he may have," the new ambassador trailed off.

Tir was angry now, obviously the old ambassador had already been bought by one of his enemies, but he could still intimidate the man, "Tell the old ambassador that if my wife is harmed by the humans, he will be held personally responsible." Then Tir dismissed them all.

He sat in his empty conference room and looked again at the article that the Galaxy Court had run about their marriage. He wondered who on his ship had told them that story? But the damage was done. Before the article had run, he had hoped to go to Earth and just convince Kara to return with him by offering her whatever she wanted, a ship, him, anything. Now, he knew he would have to bargain for her. He didn't want to have to do that, but he knew her people were holding her just for this reason alone. He was going to have to buy her and the other women like slaves and again he thought, *Why are the Lost People such barbarians?*

Kara heard someone enter the hallway that led down to her cell. As far as she knew, she and the one guard were the only ones here. She stood up to stand as close to the forcefield as she could to try and see who was walking towards her. She was very surprised to see an old Alliance man. He had grey hair to match his grey skin and a very unhappy face expression. She stood waiting and when he reached her cell he stopped and just looked at her for a good minute before speaking.

"As an Alliance citizen I am here to make sure that you are treated within reasonable comfort while incarcerated. You look okay. Are you okay?"

"Who are you?"

"I am the Alliance Ambassador Tui."

"Where is Admiral Tir?"

"He is not here."

"Seriously. You know what I meant," Kara said sharply. "Where is he?"

The old man laughed, "Young love. I remember that. Enjoy it young lady," he sighed and then said, "Your husband is on his way, no doubt to secure your release."

"How will he do that? I am going to court. I am being tried as a spy."

"Captain, no one really thinks you are a spy. You must realize that? Your government just wants better leverage when they negotiate with us about you, the other human women on the capital planet and possibly future human women going to the Alliance."

"My people are not going to auction me or anyone else off like a slave," she said defiantly. "We don't work like that."

"Yes, they are. Your government sees this as an opportunity to get military weapons, Alliance technology and universal credits. There is no doubt about it. You, being tried and convicted as a spy, only makes you more expensive."

"I don't believe you. I am an asset to my people."

The ambassador raised his eyebrows at her, "Why would I, of all people, lie to you? I am here to help you. I know your councilor. Tell her nothing. Remain silent for the next three days. Your husband is coming and the less you say, the easier this all will be." He was quiet then getting out his computer painfully slowly and grabbing a nearby chair. "I just read your reports and you said very little about your time in captivity which is good. I also have your crew's reports that basically say the same as yours. Now," he said sternly as if talking to a child, "You need just remain quiet. Do you understand?"

"Why should I believe you?"

"Has the Alliance ever done you wrong?"

"How about a forced marriage and sending half my crew off for their forced marriages?"

"Has any of your crew been forced into a marriage?"

"As far as I aware, no."

"Was your marriage really 'forced'? I have a record here from Doctor Siu as the witness who described you both as very willing on your wedding night. Are you going to dispute that? You know we have witnesses just for these purposes, so no one is forced."

Kara blushed.

"I also have receipts to show that the slave artist Sera visited you and you alone, often. I would say that you fell into Alliance life well aboard the *Refa*. Alliance clothing was bought for you, jewelry given to you, human food brought especially onboard. It does not look like there was too much 'force' involved in your marriage Captain Kara."

"You don't understand, Sera was like a friend," Kara said feeling foolish. "And I was forced to wear those clothes as the ship was so cold and they were warm."

The old ambassador wasn't having it, "No Captain Kara, slave artists are never your friends. I suspect she is actually the most probable person who sent those details to the Galaxy Court to announce your marriage. The unhappier you were are the more money she made, she probably thought it was a pity it took so long for them to publish it. But I am glad you told me that, now I understand you a bit better. As for the clothing I would say, that Admiral Tir was thinking a lot about your comfort and again, it does not come across as a forced marriage at all."

"You are twisting the facts."

"I am telling you how the rest of the galaxy sees this. Now, let me tell you how this is going to play out. Tomorrow your quick trial is going to begin. No matter what you say you will be found guilty and convicted as a spy. Then the human government has the right to keep you here incarcerated until we can seek an injunction from the Galaxy Court which would take months. But don't worry, your government doesn't want you to be incarcerated, they want to sell you. Your government recognizes that you are leaving with us, one way or another and they just want to make as much money as possible from the deal. Desperate people do desperate things and you know humans are desperate right now."

"I don't want to return with Admiral Tir. I want to live my life here, in the Terran Solar System. Where I am supposed to be. I am human."

"The moment you married, living here was never going to be an option. Even if Admiral Tir dies you are still a member of his family and are expected to live on the Alliance capital planet in his house."

"What?"

"Didn't he tell you about the Obligations and Rights of Marriage?" The ambassador answered his own question, "Of course, he didn't. I would leave you with a copy now, but I am not allowed to give you anything unfortunately. I will make sure you have a copy in English as well as our laws and everything else, so you do not have to count on your husband for information. You know Admiral Tir is a very good leader and a good man, but details do allude him occasionally." The ambassador could see this information had made her very unhappy, so he tried to cheer her up. "Everyone in the Empire is talking about his great romance with you, did you know that?"

Kara didn't speak, she didn't care. She was so angry at everything this man was telling her.

"It is said that Admiral Tir loved you from the moment he saw you and that is why he strongly insisted you marry so quickly. Now he feels completely responsible for your abduction and incarceration. Not only is he coming here to get you personally, which is something people in his position would never do, but he has also signed himself up on the Temple wall. The whole Empire is in rapture over his love for you."

"What does that mean, 'signed himself up on the Temple wall'?" She was sure this was going to be another barbaric ritual.

"He will take whatever public punishment the gods assign to him in this life for how he has mistreated you. He blames himself and his behavior for your lack of faith in your destiny together. It is a way to try and appease the gods before they give up on you both."

"Who decides this punishment?"

"The priestess will pray to the goddess for guidance and then she will tell Tir what the punishment will be."

"And this is public?"

"Yes."

"When will he do this?"

"As soon as he returns with you. He will stand before you in front of the Grand Temple and receive the punishment." The ambassador took in her slightly horrified expression. "It is his way of asking forgiveness from you and the gods. He blames himself for you ending up in this situation."

"He is right about that, it is his fault. I don't want to be his wife. I want to stay here."

"You want a lot of things you cannot have. Captain Kara, you have been given a gift, a destiny. The gods ignore most of us, but you and Tir are special. Why are you so afraid of taking the extraordinary path that has been laid before you?"

"I am not afraid, I just don't believe in this."

"What difference does belief make? The path is still there before you. You are still married to Admiral Tir, one of the most powerful men in the galaxy and he adores you. The Alliance still needs human women. I know you do not hate Admiral Tir. The whole empire had heard the rumors and reports about your romantic encounters aboard the *Refa*. And in your own personal accounts you never mentioned rape yourself, I noticed, and I do not think this is Stockholm syndrome either."

"I didn't mention the forced marriage either. Don't try to convince me I was wrong about being forced to marry of being kept as a prisoner."

"A very well looked after prisoner. Do you think I spent the last 10 years on Earth and that I don't know what humans find taboo? I know that you could never marry willingly, it is too distasteful for humans. But I also know that you would have never agreed to consummate the marriage if you did not want to either. Would you like me to read Doctor Sui's report out loud to you now?"

"No."

"I didn't think so. The gods have chosen a new life for you. It is a good life. Stop following this dream that you will always be on Earth. That future died in the war. Your new future is a good one. You like Admiral Tir, you may even grow to love him, I don't know. I know that he will not stop until he has you again." Ambassador Tui took in her unreadable face and continued, "You can become a full participant in your new life and live it to the fullest or be dragged along making each day torturous for you and Admiral Tir."

"I can't be married. I want to keep my job and my life."

"You will have a new job and a better life in the Alliance. Didn't Admiral Tir tell you that? It is in his records that he offered you a ship when you had proved yourself loyal."

"He did say that, but I thought he was lying."

"Alliance citizens rarely lie. Here is my first cultural tip for you, we will avoid the truth but not lie."

"How can I unmarry? I want to stay here."

"It is called divorce not unmarry, even though that sounds very cute when you say 'unmarry'. And unfortunately, as I said before you are going whether you like it or not. You will see tomorrow when your trial starts it doesn't matter all the good that you have done for your people. They are going to find you guilty as a spy and only grant you clemency on the terms you return to the Alliance with Admiral Tir. Don't feel sorry for yourself, most people in this galaxy have no choice about their lives, but at least your no choice is to be with a man you like and who adores you." The ambassador purposely left off saying, 'And who will be Emperor,' because he knew that kind of power and organization just scared humans. They were a very free and natural people.

"So, there are no divorces in the Alliance?""

"When you are released from this cell, I will give you a copy of the Obligations and Rights of Marriage and it will answer all of your questions. I will leave you now and remember, say nothing for the next few days. It will be easier that way. Nice to meet you Kara Zu of the Alliance. May the gods grant you wisdom."

Tir was three days away. He had received a report from the Alliance Ambassador on Earth who had seen Kara. She had been told to remain quiet about everything. Tir looked through all he could find about human laws regarding marriage and because the practice did not exist anymore, they had no laws regarding it, which was both a good and a bad thing for his position as the Alliance still saw marriage as legally binding. However, the bad part was that he was going to have to prove that she was an Alliance citizen before she became his wife and that was something that the humans were not going to like. The High Council had granted human women status as Alliance citizens three months ago, but this was for the sole purpose of solving their demographics issue and was done quietly so that firstly, there would not be a mad rush of eligible young men just going to steal a wife and secondly, so that the Galaxy Court did not immediately deem the law against the Agreement of Respect for Galactic Species. What the Alliance hoped would happen was that, human women would trickle in and it would be a natural process of integration between individuals who actually cared for one another.

Tir sighed and said out loud to no one, "And I am sorry Kara."

When Tir had read the ambassador's report he was looking for anything that would signal that she was abducted and that she did not really want to leave him, but he couldn't find anything. However, the ambassador noted that she still was wearing her marriage bracelet.

Just then his computer indicated that he had a message from his mother. He got up and went to his computer, it was a video message sent from her office. "Tir, I know you said that you were not going to leave your human with us, but I think that is foolish and I have prepared your house for her." Tir looked at the screen and thought, *Of course you have mother, let's hear it.* "I have enabled the water to go to very warm temperatures and in the bedrooms the temperature will also be able to exceed what we would find comfortable. I have also had the viewer programmed with all the entertainment from Earth which the Alliance has bought over the years. I think that you should bring her home to us and let her settle. May the gods light your journey." Tir closed his computer and went back to bed thinking about how much Kara would probably hate living on the capital planet, but he had to consider his mother's words, *Maybe she was right? Maybe Kara would have been happier there with women around her?* But that did not feel right to him, so he dismissed it again. All he wanted was for her to be back with him forever and nothing scared him more than the notion that she did not feel the same way.

Kara's councilor came back the next morning. She was wearing the same hot pink suit and lipstick. Kara wondered if it was rented and that was wearing it consecutively to get the most use out of it. Most people only owned about five complete outfits and rented the rest. Kara even owned less because most days she was wearing her uniform.

"You look tired," her councilor said disapprovingly.

"I had nightmares," Kara said getting up and standing in front of her cell waiting for the guard to release the forcefield.

Once she was out, her councilor began walking and Kara walked by her side. She noticed the councilor smelled a little bit like cigars and it pleasantly reminded her of her father, "I heard the Alliance ambassador came to see you yesterday."

"Yes."

"He even left his own guards outside so that no one would be able to get to you during the night."

"I didn't know that."

"He's not stupid," she said as they walked quickly up some stairs. "Now we are going in and all you need to say is 'not guilty'…" Kara interrupted her.

"I was told by the Alliance ambassador to say anything and I think I am going to take his advice."

Her councilor stopped walking, "Don't you want to prove your innocence?"

"I am not a spy, but since everyone already thinks that I am. I will have no chance for a fair trial anyway, you know that."

"Absolutely, but then why didn't you speak to the man behind me yesterday? Well, you are here now, we are going in, I am still making a plea for not guilty for you. If you refuse to speak, that is your right but then I will give up representing you."

"Then what will happen?"

"Honestly, I don't know. This is the most exciting thing that has happened on Earth in a long time. People are fascinated that you are married to an Alliance Admiral and half the population is convinced you are a spy and the other think you just fell madly in love with an alien and are a bit stupid." She sighed, "Listen, you have the public's ear that the government did not count on, thanks to that Galaxy Court piece on you and your husband. You know some people even say he is not bad-looking for an alien. This means, despite the outcome of your case, you will still be able to say something about what is happening, and people will be listening. These rumors about the Alliance needing women, you will have one chance during your televised trial to speak to the people."

Kara was taking all of this information in and trying to decide what she should do.

"Of course, the Alliance wants you to say as little as possible. They do not want to be incriminated for just taking human women and they want more. They are going to come here and try to negotiate that. If you say nothing, they can spin whatever story they want, and it will be too late for you to say they are lying if you try to speak after them. This is your only chance Kara to spin this the way you want people to see this."

Kara nodded, "Just promise me you will wear that same hot pink suit all the days of the trial, it gives me confidence."

"Really? This color is supposed to relax you and give you peace of mind. I promise. Now let's go in, we are already late, but it is okay because I know the judge and we were out late drinking whiskey last night at his favorite cigar bar, so he doesn't care."

Tir was two days away. The Alliance Ambassador on Earth had just sent him a message letting him know that Kara had not taken his advice and was pleading her case. There was nothing more that he could do but make sure Alliance guards were stationed outside her holding cell to make sure she was not harmed, but even that was no guarantee.

Tir left the bridge and went to sickbay to talk to Siu. He went into his office and waited for him to finish seeing a patient. When he joined Tir he asked, "What's happened now?"

"Kara is defending herself, saying she is not a spy instead of staying quiet."

"Do you think she will say that she had an abortion?"

"I don't know," Tir and Siu looked at each other seriously. In the Alliance, an abortion of a healthy fetus was forbidden and people responsible for abortions were given severe punishments that often resulted in death. "I can't tell the ambassador to tell her not to say anything and there is no way to get word to her, not that she would listen or take me seriously. I think she must be the only person I have ever met that does not take me or the Alliance seriously."

Siu smiled, "I think she takes you seriously 50 percent of the time."

Tir wanted to smile but couldn't. "I have to ask you something that has been on my mind lately."

Siu knew already what he was going to ask because he could read Tir's thoughts but allowed him to continue, as even though people knew Alliance doctors were telepathic, they didn't always like to be reminded of it.

"Do you think Kara really cares for me or was this all in my head?"

"She cares for you, there is no doubt about that. But for her marriage was so taboo, I think that was the thing that made her want to reject you. That and you probably talked about religion too much and again, for humans who abandoned religion centuries ago, it must have felt strange, almost frightening, for her."

"But it wasn't rape?"

"No."

"The ambassador has sent me a list of the crimes they are citing the Alliance for and 'the rape and impregnation' of Kara is on it. I can't help but wonder if she said that I raped her and it makes me question myself even though, logically, I know she would have said it to keep from looking like a spy, possibly..." he trailed off.

"You did not rape her Tir and if she said those things it was only to keep herself safe, which didn't work anyway. The humans just want a better deal and if Kara starts talking about forced marriages and rape, they are going to get a fantastic deal. Hopefully there will be no mention of an abortion."

"We all do," replied Tir solemnly. If it came out that Kara had willingly sought out an abortion not only would she most likely be put to death for it, the Alliance's plans of integrating with human women would be abandoned and it would be more likely that human women would just be harvested and used for their fertility like animals. The Alliance only sought to integrate human women because there was a belief that they could be civilized, if it was shown that they could not be then they would be treated as animals. He did not see any scenario where the Alliance would just leave the humans alone.

The next morning Kara found herself in court next to her councilor who was wearing the same hot pink suit and was called to the stand. Kara was asked her name and rank and how she came to find herself on the *Refa* in the first place. Then she was asked, "Did any of your crew witness this forced marriage?"

"No."

"Did any of your crew witness you agreeing to marry him?"

"Yes, through coercion. The Admiral threatened to execute my male crew if I did not marry and send my female crew to the Alliance capital planet," she was trying to stay as calm as possible.

"But did the Admiral kill anyone or just threaten to before you agreed to marry him and send your female crew away to his home planet in enemy territory?"

"No," she admitted. "However, I didn't know if he would or would not. I was not willing to risk any crew member's life to check the validity of his threat."

"Unfortunately, it just looks like you put up very little fight there to prove coercion."

"You're saying I should have let one of my crew members die to prove that I was forced to marry Admiral Tir?"

"Captain Rainer, I find it difficult to believe that you, a fearless and outstanding captain in our fleet, would have been so easily fooled unless there was something in this for you too. It just doesn't make sense. You gave not only yourself to the Alliance for months, but your female crew forever."

"In exchange for their lives, they are all still alive. Imprisoned but alive."

"That is true, but for how long and what kind of lives are those women leading in the Alliance? Are they able to freely return home? No, they are not, you sold them."

Kara looked at the prosecutor defiantly and said evenly, "I have always been loyal to Earth and would never sell one of our own."

The prosecutor knew that he had already proved his point then and the moved on, "How would you describe your time on the Alliance ship?"

"I was a prisoner."

"Really? Were you kept in the brig? Beaten? Harmed in any way?"

"No, but I was restricted to quarters with armed guards."

"Your own quarters?"

"No, I had been forced to marry Admiral Tir and so he kept me a prisoner in his quarters, none of this was my choice."

"I might believe you if you had not been found wearing an Alliance dress and jewelry and pregnant with his baby when you escaped. Do you deny any of that?"

"I was forced to do all of that."

"How many times during the war did you try and escape?"

"Many times."

"So, it is just coincidence that you escaped during the last battle? I find this difficult to believe and so do your rescuers, and I quote from Captain Jackson's report, 'It was almost too easy of a rescue from one of the Alliance's best ships. We should keep an eye on Captain Rainer as there is something here that is not right.'"

"I was only able to access communications days before I escaped. I was given more freedoms after I became pregnant."

"Yes, about that, are you still pregnant with this hybrid child?"

Kara looked at the prosecutor and said nothing. She knew this would be damning if she was.

"Captain, we are waiting for you answer."

"I sought an abortion aboard the Silverado."

"Yes, I have the report that says you went to sickbay, but I have no confirmation of what happened there. Something like a hybrid child would have been studied and there is no record of it. Are you still carrying the child?"

Kara did not speak.

"You will answer the question Captain," the judge said firmly.

"I did not have the abortion because I wanted to wait until I returned to Earth. Before I could organize it, I was arrested."

"Would you like to have the abortion now? I am sure it can be organized easily."

Kara did not speak.

"As I thought, you are reluctant to abort the child because you plan on returning to your lover. I am sorry, your husband," he spat out the words as if she had committed the most horrible crime by marrying someone.

"No, I am only reluctant to abort the fetus because it is an innocent."

"You have killed so many, it is difficult for me to believe you would want a hybrid zombie monstrosity growing inside of you if you did not love this Admiral Tir. There is no place for this child on Earth. Every patriot would kill it, yet you don't and then you sit there and have to gall to tell all of his you are not a spy."

"You don't understand." Kara felt betrayed on all sides now, but she had already been prewarned about this so she decided this was her moment to say what she needed to say and hoped she would not be silenced too soon. "The Alliance believes they can solve their demographics problem by integrating human women into their society," The judge slammed down his hammer for silence, but she ignored him and continued, "They are very religious and believe we are the same species, but what is affecting their women will kill us too."

"That is enough Captain Rainer," the judge said and motioned to the guards to take her, but Kara kept talking.

"Listen, we are all in danger. Why are you trying to confuse
people and pretend that you think I am a spy? The government
going to make a deal to ..."

Kara was led out of the room then by guards who were
covering her mouth so she could not speak. She hoped that
her outburst had been covered on the world broadcast and that
people listened to her. The guards led her back to her cell
roughly. However, when they saw the Alliance guards step forward, they were much gentler. She was left in her cell then. A
robot administered her food and water. All she could do was sit
and wait to see what would become of her.

Kara was sleeping badly, there was no window and the robot
seemed to her to come at random times with food, so she became confused about time. She tried to sleep, but it was difficult because she was haunted by her thoughts. Finally, she
drifted off to sleep thinking about whether or not Tir and the
Alliance delegation had arrived yet and then her dream took
over.

Tir was coming to get her, apologizing for everything, and
he said that she could live here on Earth and that it had all just
been a misunderstanding. When they reached her apartment,
she invited him in.

He looked around her apartment, "It looks exactly how you
said it would look."

She smiled and asked, "Is it too much red for you?"

"I don't know, I haven't seen all the rooms yet, maybe you
can show me the bedroom?"

Kara took Tir's cool, grey hand and led him into the bedroom, to her old four-poster bed with the velvet curtains and
asked, "Now what do you think?"

Tir took her in his arms then and said, "Not too much red at
all, but I am very curious how it would feel to lie down in such
an ancient bed." Then he kissed her, and she realized that she

had missed him so much then.

Kara began undressing him then and he her.

"You always look so sexy in your uniform," he said as he unzipped it.

When they had removed each other's clothing, she led him to her old-fashioned bed. She closed the heavy, velvet curtains and they were almost in the dark. "I hope you don't mind," she said in between kisses, "I don't want to give the neighbors an alien and human sex show."

"I can see in the dark just as well as in the light," Tir revealed to her and then began caressing one of her breasts so gently while he kissed her. Then his hand moved lower and began caressing her in such a familiar way, it was not long before she orgasmed, and he was slowly moving in and out of her. "I have missed you so much."

"Stay on Earth with me," she was saying in her dream and then suddenly she woke up. She was sweaty and a bit embarrassed. The robot was there delivering some food for her. She watched it and wondered if she had a fever to create such a dream. She also then wondered if Tir had been having sex with Sera while she was gone and became unnecessarily jealous, but as soon as she identified her reaction, she tried to reason with herself, *What do you care? You do not want to be married to him. You want your life back. Come on Rainer, get it together.*

But she had been told by both her human councilor and the Alliance ambassador that they could not see any scenario that she would walk out and have her old life on Earth back. That she would be sold to Tir and have to return with him. She could not help herself then and began to cry a for her lost human future and everything that had happened.

Tir and the delegation from the Alliance went down to their embassy immediately upon reaching Earth. Tir of course wanted to go see Kara directly but both ambassadors bid him wait until they had reached some agreement with the humans. He did write a note to her in Alliance though and summoned a guard to take it to her. It read,

> *Kara, I am here. You will be released today. Please say nothing more. Tir*

A few hours later, they were all sitting at a table with the humans, calmly discussing war reparations and what was to be done with the human women and as expected the humans were demanding compensation for those abducted women.

"We cannot just let you take some of our women, they can go freely of course, but to take is against Galactic Law," the president of Earth said.

The old Alliance Ambassador answered him, "First, they were taken as prisoners during war time and now, I have reports here that say the female crew from the *Dakota* that was relocated to the Alliance capital planet are happy and content to remain there and now serve with the Alliance Fleet. So, you could say they are there by their own wishes."

"Captain Rainer reported they were forced," the president said but was interrupted by Tir.

"You will refer to her as Captain Kara, she is my wife," Tir said evenly.

The president was annoyed, "Your wife, yes, the spy. She had been tried and found guilty of being a spy. I assume you think she will return with you?"

"Come president, this is all about plus and minuses. The Alliance is willing to give Earth, 700,000 universal credits, 25 model 15 laser weapons and 18 eternal batteries in return for letting the human women from the *Dakota* remain on our capital planet, the release of Captain Kara and a constant stream of human women coming to the Alliance for work, if they so choose."

The president, the vice president and the human ambassador to the Alliance all whispered together and the president replied, "For the release of Captain Kara alone we would ask for that. We need more. And a steady supply of women to create half-breeds well, we need a lot more Admiral. A million universal credits, 50 model 15 laser weapons, 20 eternal batteries, a seat on the Galaxy Court for the next twenty years and two Alpha starships."

"For that we would also require that one-hundred human fertility experts be relocated to the Alliance and we also take one-thousand human women with us now. Willingly of course," the new Alliance ambassador added.

The president of Earth looked at his team and then nodded, "Done. It will take us a couple weeks to organize..." he was interrupted by Tir.

"You have one week," Tir said sternly. "Now release my wife."

Kara heard lots of footsteps down the hallway that led to her cell. She stood up trying to see who was coming. It was a mixture of both Alliance and human guards as well as two Alliance men who were obviously officers and three humans, two who were her superiors in the fleet and one government official she had never seen before.

Kara stood up waiting to see what was going to happen.

They stopped in front of her cell, the forcefield was lowered, and one of her commanding officers began to speak formally, "Captain Kara Rainer Zu, you are formally and dishonorably discharged from the human fleet as of today. You have been found guilty of espionage. However, your prison sentence has been commuted from imprisonment in the Europa mines to banishment from Earth and all human colonies. You have one week to settle your affairs here."

Kara just looked at the General who spoke and said nothing because she was so shocked at what he had just said, even though a voice inside her head said, 'Everyone told you this was going to happen.' In those few seconds it took for the Alliance officer to stand forward she was losing her mind, trying to keep her composure then finally she asking scathingly, "What did you sell me for General? After all I have done for humans and you just sold me?"

None of her fellow humans answered her or made eye contact. They just stood there, looking everywhere but in her eyes. She was quiet then waiting to see what would happen next.

Then an Alliance officer she did not recognize stepped forward and said, "Captain Kara, you have been given a commission in the Alliance fleet under Admiral Tir that will commence after a suitable amount of training in the Empire. Now if you will come with us. We will escort you to the Alliance Embassy."

She looked at them and thought, *This is it. I have really been sold by my own people.* "Wait, I want to go home first and put my things in order."

The Alliance officer assured her that she would be able to do that afterwards and that she would be accompanied at all times by Alliance guards for her own safety.

Kara was led to the Alliance Embassy. She was led into a big room where there were five Alliance men waiting. She recognized two of them. One of the men was Doctor Siu and the other was Ambassador Tui.

Doctor Siu greeted her first, "Captain Kara, it is good to see you free and," he was holding out his scanner, "reasonably healthy." He smiled when he passed her abdomen with the scanner but said nothing more.

"Doctor, I never thought to see you again, especially under these circumstances."

"Captain Kara," Ambassador Tui addressed her. "Now that the doctor as deemed you healthy, you must take an oath to the Alliance. After all of these small formalities, you will have a week to put your affairs in order. Are you ready to take the oath?"

She looked at the old ambassador, "Yes," but could not help but think, *Please do not let it involve blood or anything barbaric.* As soon as she had thought it the ambassador brought out a sword and she knew that was not just for show. *My new people are absolute barbarians.*

"Captain Kara, take the sword in your right hand and repeat

these words to me, I Captain Kara Zu of planet Earth do pledge my life and soul to the Alliance. I solemnly vow to follow the will of the gods for the enduring survival of the everlasting Empire."

Kara took the sword and thought, *Maybe I just hold it*, "I, Captain Kara Zu of planet Earth do pledge my life and soul to the Alliance. I solemnly vow to follow the will of the gods for the enduring survival of the everlasting Empire." As soon as she had finished, the ambassador took a strong grip on both of her hands and quickly cut the center palm of her left hand with the sword. Blood dripped to the floor and someone brought a small candle so that the blood would drip on it until it was out. *And of course, there was going to be something with blood, the gods and a sword. Welcome to the Alliance Kara*, she reflected as her hand hurt.

When the candle went out it seemed to be finished. Doctor Siu came over and said, "I'm sorry I cannot heal that would as it is ceremonial and must heal according to the will of the gods."

Kara took the disinfectant gauze in his outstretched hand and held it against her left palm, "It's fine, it was just a bit of a surprise."

"I will see you aboard ship at the end of the week. Come and see me then," Siu said and then left.

"As I promised you Captain," said Ambassador Tui, handing her a small reader, "Here are the Obligations and Rights of an Alliance marriage in English, all our laws, religion and a little of our history."

She took the reader from him and thanked him. Then she was assigned two guards who escorted her back to her apartment. They waited outside her door and would presumably be there all week as she had a week to put her affairs in order.

The first thing she did was open her messages and there was one from Tir.

> *Kara, I am finishing up everything with your government and will come to you tonight for dinner. Tir*

Kara looked at the message again and began to cry. *Am I just going to accept him back?* she wondered, but then reminded herself, *He freed me, but he got me into this mess to begin with. But my own people sold me.* She thought about that for a long time. *Her people sold her.*

She hit reply.

> *Tir, as I have one week left on Earth and no food in my apartment we are not eating here. Make a reservation at the restaurant Mirazur, where our regions called France and Spain meet. The restaurant is very old, and it is legendary. You will have to bribe them, something, you no doubt are good at now. I will meet you there. Kara.*

She did not need to specify a time. Alliance people always ate at the same time, but she smiled thinking about how uncomfortable he was going to be when the meal did not end precisely after an hour. She was almost looking forward to him saying, 'This goes against the gods.'

Kara looked at the clock, she had two hours to get ready and get there by transport. She assumed that she had the use of the Alliance transport she had used with the guards to come to her apartment. She sighed and thought, *One week left on my home planet.*

After a couple sad minutes, during which time she allowed herself to uncharacteristically feel sorry for herself, she rallied and thought, *It is done. It was out of my control. I must make the best of this. My life with the human fleet and my future on Earth ended the day I was taken prisoner. I could have died. I will see it as my old self died then and this is the new me. Banished from Earth, married to an alien and pregnant with a hybrid. Why not?* Then she got into a hot shower and began thinking about what her new life would be like in the Alliance. She wondered how long she would be kept as a prisoner now that she was banished from Earth and had no job to go back to. She wondered if she should escape and become a pirate.

After her shower, she stood in front of her closet. She still had the Alliance dress that she escaped in, but as she assumed, she would have to wear one of those for the rest of her life, she opted for a human dress. She pulled out her favorite black dress, it had a collar with silver embellishments with matching embellishments on the arm cuffs and across her breasts, but her décolletage was only covered by black transparent silk. The rest of her breasts and midriff down to her thighs was covered by more embellishments and regular black silk, but after the dress reached her mid-thighs it was purely transparent black silk again down to her ankles. She wore no undergarments with this dress, not even stockings as they would take away from the flashes of flesh through the transparent sections of the dress.

When she had on the dress and looked at her appearance in the mirror, she realized that she needed some make-up too. *Why not?* she thought. *This is my last week on Earth to be completely human.* She put on smoky black eyeliner and a nude lipstick. Then she saw the barrette he had given her and put it in her hair. The only other jewelry she wore was her marriage bracelet. She looked herself over and thought, *Yes, this is how I imagine myself looking when something important happens to me. Not how I always look when important things do actually happen.*

Kara walked out her front door and the guards followed her silently. They got in the transport and she told them where to go. Once there, she told them to go find themselves some food somewhere while she ate. They refused of course but stood outside the restaurant. She knew Tir was not there yet as there was no other Alliance transport.

She walked into the beautiful restaurant and was immediately met by the hosts who were expecting her. At once she was led to a table with a stunning view of the mountains and ocean and offered her a glass of champagne while she waited. She noticed that the people around her were already whispering about her, she wanted to turn to them and say, 'Yes, it's me the spy and I am meeting my Alliance husband who bought me a couple hours ago here.' But she said nothing. She just looked at the gorgeous view and tried not to think about all the other people at the restaurant who would live out their lives on Earth. *You are saying goodbye to Earth this week. Your new life will be better than this one,* she reminded herself.

Tir was only a couple minutes behind Kara. He saw her transport there. He took a deep breath before walking in. He really did not want to meet her so publically before they had had an opportunity to talk, but he had to remind himself that she probably hated him for everything that had happened and wanted to spend as little time as possible with him privately until she was forced to, so she chose to meet at a restaurant. He had had to pay a lot of universal credits as well to get them a table, the bad publicity they said of having Kara there. He had Ambassador Tui pay them three times what they asked for just to get them to stop talking.

He walked in and was led to a table with a panoramic view of the ocean and mountains. The staff was very nice, and he thought, *As you should be considering the amount of money paid to be at this human establishment.* He did not recognize Kara at first. He had never seen her like this. He approached the table and she saw him and stood up. He was speechless. She was wearing a very sexy dress. He liked it but he definitely did not want her wearing it in public. It was so suggestive with its black transparent panels and silver embellishments, it made one think she was wearing nothing at all underneath. And she had painted her face. He had noticed that other human women did this as well, but he had never considered that Kara would do this. He found her so exotic in that moment, he did not know what to say as he looked at her.

"It would have been nice if you would have been there when I was released."

"I did not want you to say that I forced you to do anything else. You took what was offered by the Alliance freely this time," he said honestly.

"I guess I should be thanking you in a way," she said quietly.

"No Kara, you owe me nothing," he said quietly wanting to

touch her but using all of his willpower not to. In the Alliance, men and women, even married couples did not touch often in public and especially when they had an audience like now.

The hostess held out Kara's chair and she sat down again, and he sat across from her.

"You are wearing the barrette I gave you," he had not noticed before because he was so shocked by her dress and make up.

She inadvertently touched it, "Yes, I told you we would have always been lovers under different circumstances. In an alternate universe, we are lovers and live on Earth. I told you."

"And this must be our favorite restaurant," he added.

"Yes, we celebrate everything here," she said somewhat jokingly.

"I'm sorry that I was not there when you were released today and that you were imprisoned at all." He had wanted to give her time to think about everything that had happened alone, even if it was only a couple hours. And he wanted to have her make her oath to the Alliance on her own so she could not say that he hovered over her and coerced her. She could have chosen not to return to the Alliance he knew that, but he didn't think she was foolish enough to give up a command in the Alliance.

"You did warn me. I just couldn't imagine that it would turn out this way. I am not sure they would have kept in prison though if you would not have come."

"I don't want to think about what they might have done to you had I not come so quickly actually," he looked at Kara and wondered, *Are you really so naïve of the galaxy? They would have tortured you and possibly killed you trying to entice me to come negotiate your release.* "Are you okay? Nothing terrible hidden under all that face paint?"

She frowned at him, *Does he think I look bad? Is this a black lace lingerie situation?* "This," she motioned to her face, "is considered attractive on Earth. And yes, I am okay, but I am hungry."

"You are always hungry, Kara. As for the face paint, it is very attractive. Almost too attractive with the dress."

"Please do not call it face paint. It is called make-up. Face paint is what clowns wear."

"What is a clown?"

Kara just looked at Tir astonished for a second and then said, "They are terrifying creatures that live on Earth. Just be happy you've never seen one." He seemed confused but before he could ask her anymore questions the waitresses came over then and began explaining the menu. Neither one of them were listening as the spell was broken and they could hear people talking about them all around, both the good and bad.

"I will not be having the wine pairing," said Kara quietly to the waitress and she nodded. When she saw Tir's look she explained, "I don't feel like it."

"You're a terrible liar Kara," he said after a couple minutes of thinking about things. "So, we are still three at this table?"

She nodded.

"It was confusing you told me ..."

"I know what I told you. But I couldn't and now I am happy I didn't. Maybe it is good if humans have to begin conforming to galactic norms more by having to deal directly with the Alliance now." She looked at him and then admitted, "I can't believe they just sold me like that."

"Do you really want to eat here? We should go somewhere private to discuss all of this."

"Yes, I have one week before I am banished from my planet and I will have to suffer through tasteless Alliance food for the rest of my life. We are eating this food. It is some of the best in the galaxy even if no one recognizes that but humans."

He smiled at her then and remembered the day she sent her crew from the *Refa*, she had said to him that he would love Earth too in her patriotic speech to him. He reached his hand across the table and touched hers, "Kara, of course we will. I am sorry for how things happened."

After the first course she asked, "What was I sold for?"

"It was a negotiation."

She gave him a look and he continued, "Humans will have a seat at the Galaxy Court guaranteed for 20 years, some universal credits, a couple alpha ships and model 15 weapons. You were not cheap, but I would have paid much more, if you are asking?"

Hearing what he provided humbled her, "How much of it was from your own personal assets?"

"Why do you want to know?"

"I am curious because people will talk, I want to know how much the Alliance paid for human women and for me in particular."

"Half a million universal credits and my family will assure a human has a place at the Galaxy Court for you. The rest was the Empire."

Kara was speechless for a minute. Half a million universal credits was more than Earth's annual income or even ten-year income. "I am glad I know now. It makes it a bit easier."

He wanted to say, 'If you had not escaped none of this would have happened,' but he couldn't. "I know this will hurt for some time, I will try to make your transition into the Alliance smoother than before to lessen that pain at least."

Kara looked at him in disbelief was he being sympathetic, "Do you trust me now?"

"Not completely, not yet. I will still consider you my prisoner until you are holding a healthy baby in your arms."

"Please don't call me your prisoner, wife is enough."

"Kara, you will soon realize that I have always wanted just that. I don't want to have to look over my shoulder to make sure you are not running away all the time."

"That should be easier now that I have nowhere to run to."

"I want to go back to my place now."

He nodded and they left. He assumed that part of the bribery he had given the restaurant included dinner. No one stopped them on the way out. They got into his transport and flew to her apartment.

They didn't speak but she took his hand and led him into her apartment building. Once inside, she began kissing him.

She just could not help herself. *This is exactly what I missed,* she thought.

Tir's hands were on either side of her face kissing her passionately. He loved the feel of her and the smell of her. This all felt so right. It was not long before his hands began roaming over her breasts and was rubbing and pinching her nipples over the fabric. Soon, he had his hands searching for the clasps to remove her dress, but he could not find them, so after a couple minutes he took his sword and said, "I hate to do this to such a beautiful dress, but I cannot wait any longer and you will never wear it again anyway." He cut the dress off to reveal her completely naked underneath. "Gods Kara, you were completely naked under that dress? You are so naughty, come here." He dropped his sword and she went directly into his strong arms. He held her naked with her legs on his shoulders and his mouth on her vulva. "You smell so divine," he said as he began kissing her there as he held her. He made her come easily then with his hands holding her rear as he alternated between licking her clitoris and putting his tongue in and out of her vagina. After she orgasmed, he pulled his head back from gently licking her sex and asked, "Where is your bed?"

"It's in the back, behind you. The old-fashioned one there with the blue curtains," she explained.

Tir carried her in this position, her legs around his shoulders into the bedroom and then he gently laid her down on the bed, taking in her beautiful naked form and began kissing her body all over.

Kara closed her eyes and just enjoyed having him touch her again. Soon he was licking all around her upper thighs and vulva again. He was teasing her and then finally his tongue was on her clitoris, with his fingers inside of her, bringing her wet sex to climax again.

"I have missed watching you come so much. I have missed those sounds," and then she came so hard and he continued, "And your pink cheeks," his hand lightly caressed her cheek. Then he flipped her on her stomach and said, "And I have missed dominating you like you like," he grabbed both of wrists and held them behind her as he began thrusting into her. "Have you missed this?"

"Yes," she said breathlessly, and he stopped for a second. "Yes, I said. I have missed this. Don't stop now." Kara had missed this so much. He was holding her wrists and just pumping into her and she was going to come again.

Then he was coming, and they were on her bed just holding one another.

After several minutes he put his hand on one of the velvet curtains, "Your apartment is just as you described it."

"I want to stay here this week. You don't have to if you find it too primitive."

"It is primitive, but I would like to stay with you. I know this week will be difficult. You will need to say goodbye to everyone."

Tears began streaming down her face then, "I can't believe I am banished." She said to his naked grey chest as he held her close.

"I know but they couldn't find you guilty as a spy and then just let you go serve in the Alliance without any kind of punishment, could they? You know your people. I tried to say that you could have escaped or something, but they would not have it. It had all become too public." He ran his fingers through her hair, "I promise you I will make this up to you."

His last words reminded her of something Ambassador Tui had mentioned to her, "What is this about you putting your name on the Temple wall?"

"To make things right with the gods and you." He put his hand on her abdomen and then said, "And I am so glad you are still pregnant. I was so afraid that you would have or been forced to abort the child."

"I thought about it, but I couldn't. I guess I am really a traitor in that way, I may be destroying humanity by doing this, but they just sold me, so I guess I have no allegiance anymore to my own people." She tried to hold back more tears then while she